JOHN HEARNE

SOMEONE'S BEEN MESSING WITH REALITY

GW00762769

Little
Island
Books create waves

PRAISE FOR

THE VERY DANGEROUS SISTERS OF INDIGO McCLOUD

by JOHN HEARNE

'Hilarity and heart center this quirky story about a young hero quietly taking a stand.'
Kirkus Reviews

'An exciting and original debut.'
The Irish Times

'A raucous read with notably Roald Dahl–leaning social sensibilities.'
Publishers Weekly

'This Irish import will please children who want an over-the-top bully book jam-packed with adventure. This novel is wacky, awesome, and terrifying.'
School Library Journal

'Writing a dystopian world that is laugh-out-loud funny is no mean feat, but to create such an environment for young readers is nothing short of extraordinary.'
Inis magazine

'Descriptive and quirky.'
LoveReading4Kids

'A sure hit for readers who like nothing more than the sort of outrageous adventure that only a wild imagination can deliver. Perfect for the reader on the verge of becoming addicted to reading for life!'
School Library Connection

'Missing Roald Dahl? Need a book where bad kids are just bad and they get their comeuppance? This is the book for you. John has written a fabulously funny, dark, clever novel.'
Read and Reviewed

'Quirky, humorously sinister and thoroughly entertaining.'
Fallen Star Stories

'What a delightfully twisted book! The story is unpredictable and keeps the readers at the edge of their seats. It oddly reminds me of a Tim Burton movie, dark, but Indigo is rather lovable unlike the rest of his family.'
NetGalley Reviewer

SOMEONE'S BEEN MESSING WITH REALITY

First published in 2024 by
Little Island Books
7 Kenilworth Park
Dublin 6w
Ireland

© John Hearne 2024
The author has asserted his moral rights.

All rights reserved. No part of this book may be reproduced, trans-
mitted or stored in a retrieval system in any form or by any means
(including electronic/digital, mechanical, photocopying, scanning,
recording or otherwise, by means now known or hereinafter invented)
without prior permission in writing from the publisher.

A British Library Cataloguing in Publication record for this book is
available from the British Library.

Cover design by Dan Bramall
Copy-edited by Emma Dunne
Typeset by Rosa Devine
Printed in Poland by L&C

Print ISBN: 978-1-915071-48-4
Ebook ISBN: 978-1-915071-67-5

Little Island has received funding to support this book from
the Arts Council of Ireland/An Chomhairle Ealaíon

10 9 8 7 6 5 4 3 2 1

For Marie

1. VIDEO

Before the second fall, before the mayhem in the quarry, before the Battle of the Turtle and everything that happened after that, there was Dad, hanging by his fingers from the gutter at the back of the house.

Picture him there, six metres in the air: arms extended, hands clinging. You can see the shiny dome of his head, rimmed by neat black hair. You can just see the backs of his glasses hooked over his slightly sticky-out ears. He's wearing a short-sleeved check shirt, cargo shorts and sensible working boots.

His calves are exceptionally hairy.

Our house backs onto the woods, and we have no near neighbours, so no-one can see him. He could call out to my mother, who's the only person within earshot. She's in their bedroom, packing a case. They're both due to go away for the night, leaving me on my own for the first time ever. But he's not calling to her; he's not calling to anybody. It's hard to tell from this angle – you can't see his face – but he actually doesn't seem too troubled by his situation.

So let's just leave him there for a minute.

***

About the same time that he's dangling above our path, Tina and Enda and I are freewheeling down the hill to the village. Cycling is about the only thing that Enda can still do the same as before. He's standing on the pedals and flying down the road ahead of us. From behind, everything is just the same. It's like last year or the year before. I feel the air on my face and the speed of the bike underneath me and it's summer and there's no school. I know nothing about Dad's predicament, not yet, and so for a minute, I forget about everything bad. Then Tina starts singing 'We're Not Gonna Take It' by Twisted Sister. She can't sing a note. Neither can I, so I join in and now we're both singing at the tops of our lungs.

It's the Friday of Spacer Weekend, the biggest weekend of the year in Glencooper. Hordes of sci-fi heads, cosplayers, traders, hippies, bikers, campers and assorted eccentrics descend on the place and turn it from a sleepy little seaside village into the kind of place where anything can happen. We zip into the village underneath a huge banner they've stretched across the road. 'Welcome to Glencooper UFO Festival!' It's decorated with poorly drawn figures: R2-D2, Groot, some anonymous dude in a spacesuit and a Mr Spock that looks a lot more like Elrond.

The place is packed. There are about fifteen Harleys lined up outside Flannery's pub, and a mix of Jawas, Ewoks and Wookiees are playing basketball in the courts across the road. Benny Doyle has his booth up outside Russo's takeaway and is busy taking bookings for his daily UFO tours. In the little arcade between Russo's and the Spar, kids are busy at the machines. Music is pumping out, and underneath it you can hear the squirrelly sounds of aliens being destroyed in a game of *Space Invaders*. We turn in to the car park by the beach and dodge a Mandalorian shaving at the wing mirror of his camper van. Darth Vader and Princess Leia go by hand in hand while a stressed-out Thor, sweating under a huge red robe, is trying to put sun cream on a wriggling toddler.

As we're parking the bikes, I break it to Tina that my mother made me promise that I wouldn't go swimming while they were away and that I'd be home by nine.

She stops what she's doing and stares at me like I've just told her that Christmas is cancelled.

I throw my arms wide. 'They made me! If I didn't promise, they would have called the whole thing off.'

'Home by nine? What age does she think you are? Five?'

'We can still hang out,' I say. 'We can still stay up late and watch something. We can check the trail cams.'

We'd put up trail cameras in the woods at the back of my house, hoping to get footage of owls or pine martens or something. I'm doing my best to make this sound more exciting than a midnight beach party. Tina isn't going for it.

'I mean, what does she think you'll do, exactly?' she says. 'It's not as if you ever put a foot out of line. I don't understand why she doesn't trust you.'

'It's not that she doesn't trust me, it's just –'

'And no swimming? What's that about? They treat you like a baby and you just take it, you just … God, Martin, are you even listening?'

'I'm listening, I'm listening. I just can't see him, T.'

I always get jumpy when Enda wanders off. I mean, he's never disappeared or anything, but I'm still worried it'll happen when we're supposed to be minding him.

'Give him a break, will you?' she says. 'You watch him like your parents watch you.'

'Yeah, but where is he?'

'There!'

She points to where he is standing at the low wall that borders the car park and the beach. He's looking up at the sky. This is unusual. Most of the time he either wanders off down the beach or just stands there, head bent, zoned out, like he doesn't know or care where he is.

'It's an unreasonable demand!' she goes on. 'It's a promise extracted under duress. Promises extracted under duress don't count, they –'

Next thing her face breaks into a smile at something behind me. Before I can turn around I'm in a headlock.

A deep voice: 'Guys! Come on! It's Spacer Weekend and you're fighting? Not cool!'

It's Cool Billy. He's back. He spins me round then lets me go.

'It is good to see you, Ms O'Reilly.' He lifts the bucket hat from his straw blond hair and bows deeply to Tina, who's grinning madly. They do the handshake he taught us.

Holly comes up and slips her arm around Billy's waist. She's smiling her 400-watt smile and is wearing a bikini top with some kind of a sarong thing.

'When did you get here?' I ask.

'Mr Martin Ryan, sir!' Billy salutes; then we do the handshake. 'The wisest man in Glencooper. Just last night! It's good to see you guys. How've you been?'

'Bored,' says Tina. 'Have you been surfing yet?'

'Couldn't go without you,' says Holly.

Holly and Cool Billy. Our favourite spacers. They spend most of the year wandering around Europe in a Volkswagen van, but they never miss this weekend.

Everything about Billy is bigger and brighter and louder and faster than the rest of the world, but really, I've been dreading their arrival. And I don't know how Tina isn't. Because he doesn't know about the fall. He doesn't know what happened.

And now, of course, he looks around and goes, 'Where's Enda?'

***

We get back to the house at 8.53. It's empty, just as I expected it to be. I don't yet know about Dad and the gutter. I don't yet know how he got down from there. All that sits lurking in the future.

Mam's note is two pages long and covers such diverse topics as the safe operation of the cooker, the importance of bicycle helmets, the dangers of mineshafts (long story) and the terrible consequences of talking to 'the oddballs that show up at this time of year'.

My phone beeps me awake at 11.20pm. It's Mam:

I hope you're in bed.

I'm on the couch. On the TV, Smaug sweeps low over Lake-town. Tina is stretched out on the rug, dead to the world.

Enda didn't stay over. His mam likes him home before it gets dark.

***

When we check the trail cams the next day, one of them has come loose and is dangling by one strap from one of the trees closest to the garden. It's now pointing at the back of our house.

'Gah!' says Tina. 'That's your fault.'

This is true. I was in a bit of a hurry when I was putting it up. I'm not crazy about heights and I wanted to get back down the ladder fast, so I didn't bother tying the second strap.

All of the cameras have night vision and are motion activated, which means you don't have to sit through hours of empty footage waiting to see if anything showed up. Three of the five cameras have recorded something, but that includes the one that spent the last twenty-four hours pointing at the back of the house.

There's thirty seconds of footage on the first one, triggered by a pigeon that sweeps past in the first half second. Then nothing, just the eerie infra-red darkness where the tree branches look like bones.

We're up in my room, hovering over my laptop.

I hook the second camera up to the computer and download all of the footage. There are three separate videos on this one. One is twenty-three minutes long, one five and the last one seventeen. This is promising. We take the longest first.

There's the same weird monochrome light, making the trees look like something out of a horror film. We're both staring at the screen, trying to see what triggered the sensor.

'What's that there?' T points to a shadow on the ground.

'Dunno, just ferns or a rock or something.'

We stare unblinking at the screen for the full twenty-three minutes before it goes black. Whatever triggered the camera didn't stick around. But on the five-minute one, something we can't see is making the branch move. It stays stubbornly out of shot.

'Come on!' Tina shouts at the screen, which then goes black. 'Gah!'

The last piece of footage was taken only about half a minute after the previous one ended. It's the same branch, jerking up and down erratically.

Then we see it. A tail? No, but definitely something moving, something animal.

A quiet buzz at my wrist: my meds alarm going off.

'Time for your medication, Mardy,' says Tina, in a New York accent.

I have a rare blood disease, so rare it doesn't have a name. It's a version of polycythaemia vera, or PCV, where the body makes too many red blood cells. Doesn't bother me, doesn't stop me doing anything. The only drag is the medication. Three pills, five times a day. I've got a little watch that vibrates when it's pill time. The aspirin is easy to take, but the two big grey ones are hard to swallow – literally. Sometimes I need three or four goes. Sometimes they make me throw up. Every three months, Mam does blood tests – she's a doctor – but, like I say, I've been fine. There's nothing I can't do.

I slip out and take the pills. I don't like taking them when anyone's watching. When I get back, Tina is peering at a corner of the screen, 'Is that a nose?'

There's just the tiniest tip showing, right at the edge. Then it scuttles out onto the branch and there it is in all its glory. A rat.

'Oh, for God's sake,' says Tina, throwing herself back in the chair.

'Who knew they could climb?' I say.

'Here,' she says, getting up, 'we might as well check the last one. It might not have slipped down until morning.'

She hooks up the camera to the computer.

Out the window, I see Enda arriving into the back garden. He doesn't come into the house but heads straight for the shed. Since the accident, he spends hours and hours in there, watching Dad's model trains going round and round and round. He never moves them from one track to another, or reverses the trains or anything, never re-arranges the carriages or the tiny people in the little model town. He just sits there, staring, like a cat watching a washing machine.

There's a snort laugh from Tina behind me. 'Your dad, cleaning the gutter.'

I come round and see him at the top corner of the screen, digging shovelfuls of sodden leaves out of the gutter and dumping them into a yellow bucket looped by its handle around the top of the ladder.

Tina does a David Attenborough voice. 'Every year, without fail, at the exact same time, this strange creature emerges from its den and completes this same peculiar ritual. Observe its curious plumage.' She laughs, and in her own voice, she says, 'I see he's ditched the socks-and-sandals combo for the hiking-boot look. Oh!'

I've drifted to the window but a crash from the computer brings me back. Dad is dangling from the gutter. The ladder has fallen. The bucket full of leaves is broken on the ground.

The sight of him two storeys above the ground makes me feel slightly ill.

'This was yesterday afternoon,' says Tina. 'Is he OK?'

'Well, yeah, I mean, we were at the beach when they left, but they got off OK. Mam texted half a dozen times. She never mentioned this.'

'So how did he get down?'

He's dangling there for ages. He's not calling out; he's not screaming for help.

'Not exactly panicked, is he?' says Tina.

Next thing he lets one hand go, so that now he's dangling there by his left hand. I bring my hands to my face. I can't look at this. But, but, but, he reaches up, feels around in the gutter, finds the little shovel and scoops out the last of the wet leaves.

'What?' says Tina.

Next thing, my father takes one last awkward look around, then lets go of the gutter completely and floats gently to the ground, as if he's Mary Poppins and the shovel full of dead leaves is a magic umbrella.

2. F35

Tina jumps up like the chair is on fire. It goes spinning back against the bed. On the screen, Dad is picking up the broken pieces of yellow bucket. There's no audio but he looks like he's whistling.

'How?' she says. 'Did you see that?'

I nod. It's all I can do.

Dad is looking around. He stares for a moment into the trees at the bottom of the garden. Next thing the fallen leaves – the wet leaves that spilled out of the broken bucket – fly up into the air, like a swarm of insects, and hover there in front of him. Then they go shooting down the garden towards the camera. Except they don't move like insects. They travel in perfectly straight lines, like a squadron of fighter planes. We can see them clearly as they come to the edge of the wood, where they stop suddenly and flutter to the ground just in front of the camera. Dad's left the shot.

Tina looks at me. 'You're having a laugh, right? This is some kind of joke, right?'

I grab the mouse and pull the cursor back. We both stare silently at the screen, as once again my dad, my forty-seven-year-old, bald, moustachioed dad, wearing cargo shorts and check shirt, dangles from the gutter, then lets go and floats gently to the ground. Floats. Gently. To. The. Ground.

Tina goes to pull back the cursor again.

'Wait,' I say. 'I want to see the leaves.'

Just like before, Dad picks up the bucket and looks around.

'He's checking to see if anyone's watching,' I whisper. 'He's checking to see if the coast is clear.' The leaves rise into the air and zip towards us. This time I keep my eyes on Dad. He watches them as they fly down the garden, then turns away as soon as they're in the trees, as soon as they're clear of the lawn. Right then, right at that moment, he turns away, and the second he does, the laws of physics kick back in. The leaves float to the ground.

'Martin.' Tina's hands are in her hair, grabbing bunches of it. 'What is that – what's going on?'

I pull back the cursor again. This time I stop it as he's halfway down. He's frozen there, three metres above the ground.

Tina gets between me and the screen. 'Do you know anything about this? If this is some kind of joke –'

I shake my head.

'Can you do that?'

I keep shaking my head.

'Your mam?'

I stop shaking my head. 'You're asking me if my mother can fly?'

Tina has to double-check with her brain. She nods.

'I don't think so. I mean, not as far as I know.'

We replay the footage again and again. There are no wires floating him to the ground. No safety harness, no jetpack, nothing. It's just Dad. Good old Dad. Solid, dependable Dad. Chock-full of good advice that's kind of hard to follow. A bit goofy. Eats ice-cream cones from the bottom up. Likes fart jokes. Dad. Not Clark Kent or Dumbledore or Gandalf or Iron Man.

Dad.

I replay the video again, this time at half speed. Then at quarter speed. Then at double speed. I don't know why I'm doing any of these things. Maybe if I keep looking at it, keep messing with it, we'll suddenly see something we've been missing. I keep expecting Tina to punch me in the shoulder and say something like, 'Martin, you gom, you accidentally turned off the gravity.'

'When are they home?' she asks.

'Mam's due back at two. Dad said he'd be a bit later.' She's at a conference. He's at some kind of work thing too. I try to remember what. A seminar? What even is a seminar? I pick up my phone and call Mam. She doesn't answer. I picture her, sitting in a big room full of people, her phone vibrating silently in the bag hanging on the back of the chair. I call Dad's phone but that goes straight to his message minder.

Tina's sitting on the bed. Perfectly still, perfectly quiet. This doesn't happen much.

'What?' I ask.

'You really don't know anything about this?' she says.

'About ... about my father flying?' The words, when I hear them out loud, almost make me laugh.

'This isn't some kind of show you're putting on,' she says, 'pretending to be surprised because I've found out?'

'No.'

I jump back onto the computer. 'This is stupid. The thing must be glitching. It must be.' Over the next hour we go over the footage frame by frame. We download video analysis software and run the file through it. That turns up nothing. I take the camera and hook it up to the desktop in the study downstairs, but that doesn't reveal anything either.

The phone is hardly out of my hand, but the call back I'm waiting for won't come. Each time I have to wait for something to load or power up, I try one of their phones. Hers rings and rings and rings. Could she be sitting there still? Staring up at somebody on the stage talking about kidneys or livers or sore knees or something? If she was planning to be home by two, then she'd have to be on the road by now, and she's got hands-free in the car. Now I get a stab of guilt. She'll get the fright of her life when she sees thirteen unanswered calls.

I'm sitting on the bed, head in my hands, while Tina paces up and down. She's like a lawyer in a TV movie, putting her questions to the defendant. 'This can't be the only time, Martin, it can't be. Think!'

Dad's phone is still off. I try to convince myself that there's nothing unusual in this. He's still in meetings or talks or something. He's still –

'Martin!' Tina clicks her fingers in front of my face.

'God. What?'

'This has to have happened before. Think back, has he, has she …?' Tina goes still.

'What?'

'Dan Brolly's little brother.'

'Dan Brolly's brother? What has he got to do with –? Oh.' Oh.

So we were in the car. I was in the passenger seat. Tina and Enda were in the back. Four years ago? Five? Mam was driving. We must have been dropping Tina home or something, because we were going up the hill on the school road. We were eating Tic Tacs – I remember that. Just beyond the turn to Oak Tree Heights, Mam brought her foot down hard on the brake and the car jerked to a stop. We all had safety belts on, but we were still thrown forward.

'Hey! What are you doing?'

She didn't reply. She spun the wheel and accelerated into the estate. There was a truck. One of the big ones that delivers heating oil. It was stopped at an angle, half blocking the road. Someone was running from the nearest house towards it.

Enda got it first. 'There's been an accident.'

Mam pulled up and turned around to look at us. 'Nobody leave this car, do you understand me?'

Enda's hand was already on the handle of the door. 'But, Helen, you know I want to be a doctor, I really think that –'

'Enda. No. Stay.' My mother had a look in her eyes, one that I rarely saw and that Tina and Enda had never seen before. 'Do you understand me?'

They nodded rapidly. Next thing she was out the door. She got the big brown doctor bag she always keeps in the boot and ran towards the oil tank. Ran. Mam never runs. There were more people there now. I recognised Mrs George and one of the Power twins – Clodagh. She turned from the truck and threw up. Mrs George had her hands over her eyes, and next thing Dan Brolly's mother comes sprinting from one of the houses, screaming.

And then, right then, that's when the oil tanker lurched to the side. It jumped sideways. Jumped. This was not a manoeuvre that anyone driving the thing could have made.

'Did you see that?' said Enda. 'Did you see that?'

But now we could see the little legs sticking out from under it, and Mam bent over the little body, and that sight, that blew everything else away.

He died, Dan Brolly's little brother. There was nothing Mam could do. And for weeks, the whole place was in this fog of sorrow, and that's probably why we never really talked about the oil truck.

'She made that truck move with her mind, Martin.'

'Just slow down a sec, Tina.'

'You saw it, I saw it, Enda saw it. They can both do it, Martin, both your parents.'

'Just because, I mean, she never, like, well …'

'Go on,' says Tina.

My meds alarm goes off and I reach into my pocket for the pills. For once I don't leave the room to take them. Being shy about them suddenly seems stupid. I would have expected Tina to look away or something. She knows I don't like taking them in front of people. Instead she stares – I mean really stares. She watches my hands as I pop open the blisters and place the three pills – one small and white, two large and grey – on the desk. I get the water bottle and swallow them down one by one.

'What?' I say. 'Seriously, Tina, what is it?'

Out on the road, a motorbike roars by.

'Why yesterday?' she says. 'Why did they go yesterday?'

'My parents? I told you. Work stuff.'

She dives for the computer and starts hammering on the keyboard. *Where are they?* This is all I can think. *Where are they?* It's a nice simple puzzle, with a nice simple answer, right? And it keeps my mind off the bigger one. *What* are they? Because now a whole pile of memories are tumbling down on top of me, and I'm trying to keep them off by thinking ordinary things, like they forgot their chargers or Dad dropped his phone in the toilet and Mam is just so caught up in talking about livers or sore knees that she didn't manage to leave when she had planned. Dad'll come rolling in any second and take one look at that video and laugh and say … and say …

I can't sit still for long. I get up and go to the window. Enda's looking up at me from the middle of the garden. I do a double take. He's standing there staring right into my face. This hasn't happened since the fall. He hasn't met my eyes in eight months.

I wave down. 'Tina, look.' But he turns away, back towards the shed.

She's started reading something aloud. '"Witnesses at several coastal locations recount seeing a dark object in the air over the sea between 8.15 and 8.23 on the evening of 23 June 2006."'

I realise what she's doing. 'Oh, come on, Tina. Seriously?'

'"The object appeared to be travelling inland, and was last seen between the village of Glencooper and Knocknagown Woods at 8.23pm. It was described as oblong in shape and either black or navy blue in colour."'

'You really don't expect me to believe that –'

She holds up a hand. '"While the object was never formally identified, it is known that test flights of the Royal Air Force prototype F-35 were conducted in this area. Sightings of the F-35 have explained similar unidentified flying objects off the North Sea coast of Scotland."'

She turns away from the screen and starts talking fast, more to herself than me. 'It's pretty lame, really, isn't it? I mean, all it says is that it might have been a plane. I never thought it was enough to base a whole festival on – I mean, I always assumed the UFO spotters were the idiots, but ...' She looks up at me, then gets mad. 'Come on, Martin. Say something!'

But it's like I can suddenly feel the planet spinning beneath my feet. 'They met in Dublin.' I don't know why

I've landed on this but I have. 'She was working in the emergency department in the Mater Hospital. He cut his finger opening a can of beans and came in to have it stitched. They celebrate on that date every year. They call it their anniversary. They always have baked beans.' I look at Tina. 'Do you think that's true? Do you think that happened?'

She starts to say something, then stops.

'I always have fish fingers,' I say. 'I don't like baked beans.'

'You have no other family, Martin,' she says. 'Grandparents? Dead. No aunts, no uncles. They're both only children, your parents. Do you get how unusual that is? And they arrived down here from – where was it? Antrim? And you never go there, you never go back there. Why? Because there is no back there. None of it is real. Oh my God, Martin.' Now her own logic seems to overwhelm her and she jumps up. 'Oh my God, Martin.'

'It can't –'

'They've no accents, Martin. They're from the north and they don't have accents.'

'It doesn't … I can't …'

'All right then, what? What? I'm all ears.'

I'm shaking my head, which is a bad idea, because I dislodge one of those memories, one of those dangerous memories.

'My appendix,' I say.

Tina narrows her eyes, not getting it. Then she gets it and her eyes get so big. 'Oh my God, your appendix!'

My appendix got inflamed when I was nine years old. I had pain in my side. Mam diagnosed it, then, with Dad's help, she operated on me here in the house. She told me that it had burst, that it was too late to get to hospital. She said if she hadn't done what she did, I'd have died. I remember very little about it except a lot of pain and a lot of drifting in and out of consciousness in a room bright and white as a laboratory.

'She couldn't let any other doctor see you. Because …' Tina looks at my stomach, 'because you're … different.'

'But I was in hospital when I was three or four. For ages.'

'You remember that?'

'Well, no, but … She told me about it …'

'What else, what else, Martin? You're remembering other things, aren't you? Come on.'

Here they come, all of them, here they come.

'On Christmas Day, she was taking the turkey out of the oven and it fell, or at least I thought it fell – she was lifting it up and she didn't have a good grip on it but she managed to catch it. I remember blinking, I remember thinking that was weird. It's like it slowed down in mid-air, slowed down enough for her to catch it. God!' I slap my forehead. 'Mam does it all the time. Why didn't I see this before? She does it all the time. She parks the car crooked, but when we come back, it's exactly between the lines. I never said anything about it. I always thought, oh, she's better at parking than I thought, but, but she just,

she always just ...' I flop down on the bed again. 'What
am I?'

Pause.

'You're an alien, dude.'

3. FALL

So it was a Wednesday in October. Last October. Cold and windy and bright. This isn't me with a weather report. The wind, that was part of it. It was after school and the three of us were freewheeling down past the old mineshafts to the cliffs at Annestown. Enda was singing. He was always singing, even though he couldn't sing any better than me and Tina. He loved those big eighties anthems, especially 'We're Not Gonna Take It'. By then, Tina and I had heard him sing the song so often we knew it by heart, so we joined in.

We dumped the bikes on the road and headed up along the rabbit runs towards the highest point of the cliffs. There's not much shelter around there. The wind tears in from the sea and everything that grows is crooked.

'It's going to rain,' said Enda, marching ahead of us.

'Hardly,' said Tina.

He pointed at the sky, at the lines of jagged, dirty-looking cloud. 'Cirrocumulus,' he said, 'specifically stratiformis undulatus. Mackerel sky, mackerel sky, never long wet and never long dry. Sign of a change in the weather.'

Enda liked clouds. These days, he hardly ever looks up, but back then, he used to walk with his head tilted upwards, light glinting off his glasses. Now, he doesn't even wear the glasses any more. Why is that?

'Don't look much like mackerel to me,' said Tina.

'Ah, but you see, T, you're used to the Atlantic mackerel,' he said, turning back to her. 'The lad after which this sky is named is the king mackerel, a migratory species more likely to be found in the Gulf of Mexico. Take a look at that lad's markings and you will see –' He turns back and points without looking at the sky. 'And you will see that.'

The further we got from the road, the more wild and empty the landscape got. It was just heather now, rough and springy, with a narrow track curving through it. The sea was below us to the left. To our right, the land swept upwards with nothing but the odd rock or sheep. You couldn't see anything man-made. It was just the same as it was a thousand years ago. As we got higher, another clump of cloud came into view.

'What type are they, then?' I asked.

'Fluffy ones!' he shouted over the wind.

Tina snort-laughed.

'Stratus,' he said, shoving the glasses back up his nose. 'Stratus nebulosus. Nastiest of clouds. Full of the rain the cirrocumulus promised.'

'Maybe we should head back,' I said.

'Nah, we've got half an hour yet.'

I hung back and took my four o'clock meds. I had enough water for these, but not, I now saw, for the next set. Unlikely, I figured, that I would need to take them outside. It'd be well dark by then. We'd surely be home.

They were waiting for me up ahead on the path. Enda lifted his glasses and looked at me. 'OK?'

'Yeah. Just … you know … the meds.'

He didn't say anything but continued to stare.

'What?'

When he started to say something Tina was suddenly impatient. 'Come on if we're going.' She grabbed his coat and pulled him after her. I ran to keep up. She was leaning towards him, saying something I couldn't hear.

'What? What's going on?'

Enda spun round. He was grinning. 'I want to try something.'

That's important. For both of us, for me and Tina. It was his idea. Not hers. And not mine. Never mine.

The cliffs at Annestown are 110 metres above the water, but the water at the base is fairly shallow, even at high tide. There's a thick shelf of rock that runs along this section of coast, so cliff diving is out. Plus the cliffs themselves aren't sheer. There are ridges and outcrops and things most of the way down. Sheep are always getting stuck on them. In the summer, we often come up here. Tina and Enda used to lie on the grass on their bellies and stare down at the waves battering themselves to foam at the base of the cliffs. I could never do that. Three metres, that's as close as I come. The thought of looking over the edge gives me the screaming heebie-jeebies. But this wasn't the summer; this was October and the grass was wet and no-one was lying on anything.

Enda strode up to the edge. He planted his feet right there, right on the very edge. Then he opened his coat wide, holding the lower edges so that it was like a pair of wings. Then he leaned out.

'Enda! Stop! Come back!'

He roared into the wind – something I couldn't hear – and only leaned out further and balanced there, the wind pushing him back. The sight of it made me sick.

'Enda, come on!'

Next thing Tina ran up beside him, opened up her coat and did the same thing.

'Tina!'

I wanted to grab them both by their coats and drag them in, but I was afraid if I went near them, I'd somehow push them over. They both leaned out so far that it almost looked like they were no longer touching the ground, like they were gulls hovering right at the edge.

'Guys, please! Come on!'

Tina was screaming. Enda was still shouting something I couldn't hear. All the strength was gone out of my fingers, my legs, my arms.

'That's ENOUGH!'

Tina heard the panic in my voice, stepped back and turned, face red, grinning. 'Martin, you've got to try this, it's –'

And then the wind died. It just died. And Enda was gone.

***

Eight o'clock. Six hours after Mam said she'd be home. No sign of either of them. No call, no text, nothing. I go through Mam's stuff and find the name of the hotel the conference is in. The guy on the reception desk says he'll put me through to her room, and I hover there for what feels like six months, listening to hold music. I keep imagining it stopping suddenly and her voice, calm and warm, singing out. 'Hi Martin! Everything OK?'

But in the end, the receptionist comes back. 'Sorry, Dr Ryan checked out this morning.'

So I tell him it's an emergency and I ask him to page her, and again, I'm holding my breath, listening to the plinky-plonky music, expecting her voice, breathless on the line. 'What's wrong, Martin? Are you OK?'

Eleven minutes and forty-seven seconds later, the same guy is back. 'I'm sorry, she must have left.'

I can't find any record of Dad's seminar at home, but this isn't surprising. He's got an office thirty kilometres away, on the outskirts of the city, and he rarely brings work home. An online search for civil-engineering seminars doesn't turn up anything. His office phone is diverted to his mobile. So I'm straight to his message minder, except now the voice says, 'This person's mailbox is full. You cannot leave a message.' Next I try Sorcha, the woman who does admin work for him, but her phone is off too.

So the most in-touch, tell-me-your-every-move, text-me-when-you-get-there parents on the planet have disappeared.

I call the cops.

That's what you do, isn't it? When people go missing? The cops are really nice. They take me dead seriously and take lots of details about what they look like, the hotel Mam was staying at and the types of cars they were driving and all that. I stay on the line while the woman 'checks the system'. Five minutes later, she says that there have been no reports of any accidents involving their cars. She tries to be reassuring and talks about breakdowns and forgetting chargers in hotels and all of the things I thought of hours ago. She asks me if I'm on my own and I tell her no, that I'm staying with a friend tonight.

'Is there anything else I should know?' she asks.

Yes, well actually, since you ask, it turns out they're aliens. Not sure where they're from exactly – only just figured it out. Bit of a coincidence? I find out they're extra-terrestrial and they disappear. Yes, indeed, isn't it just?

'No thanks,' I say.

As soon as I finish the call, the phone beeps, but it's just Enda's mam. She checks in three or four times a day. I text her back rapidly. *All well, will have him home by 9.* I add three smiley faces and two thumbs up. In the early days, when he came back from the rehab place and she let him out with us for the first time, I had to keep reassuring her he was fine. Nothing says your brain-damaged son is safe with me like three smiley faces and two thumbs up.

Tina comes back into the kitchen from upstairs. 'What did the cops say?'

I fill her in. Then I say, 'I'm an idiot. I mean, fourteen years, nearly fifteen years, I've lived with these people and never once twigged it.'

'I called it.'

'Shut up, Tina.'

'I said it, don't you remember? I said it. I said, "Your father is so ordinary, he has to be a serial killer or an alien or something." It's like someone gave him a guide on how to act like an Earth da. I bet he has a copy of it somewhere upstairs. The clothes and the moustache and the lawn and the DIY. I mean, even his job. Engineer has to be the most da job ever.'

'He's more than that,' I say. 'He's not a joke.'

'I know. Sorry.'

Silence.

'What are they doing here?' I ask.

'What are they doing here? You mean why did they come here?'

'Yeah.'

She looks at me funny.

'What?'

'Well, you know what I –'

But my meds alarm goes off again. I dig in my pockets but I'm all out so I head upstairs to get a fresh box out of the bathroom. I scan the cabinet up and down but it's empty. Odd. Could have sworn there were three or four boxes in there. Tina appears in the doorway. She's got the same weird look on her face. I stop dead.

'Tina,' I say slowly, 'what have you done?'

'Trust me on this,' she says, holding up her hands.

'Tina!'

I run into my parents' bedroom. The packs Mam buys wholesale are sitting in the bottom of the wardrobe. Or at least they should be. All that's left is the cardboard box. It's empty.

'Tina!'

She's still in the bathroom when I get back there. And now I see what I missed the first time. The bath is full of boxes of Hydroxithon – the big grey pills I have to take five times a day. I swoop and pick one up. It's empty. So is the next one. It's not just empty boxes. There are empty blister packs everywhere. The inside of the toilet bowl is covered in a grainy pink residue. The water is pink and frothy.

'Tina! What did you do?'

She's turned and is skipping down the stairs. I dive among the boxes and blister packs but can't find a single pill. Downstairs I hear a toilet flushing and run down to find Tina standing in the hall with an empty pill box in her hand.

'I forgot the ones in the camping gear in the kitchen,' she says. 'They're all gone now.'

'Tina! Why? Why?'

'Martin, come on, think about it.'

'I don't know where she gets them.' I'm pacing, talking frantically to myself. 'She gets them online. I don't even know where. She orders them about once a year. They arrive by courier.'

'Listen to yourself, Martin, listen. *You* don't know where she gets them. *She* orders them once a year. Martin. You're not sick. You don't have a rare blood disorder. There's nothing wrong with you. They give you those pills to stop you from being able to do … what your dad did.'

'I could die, Tina. I could die without those drugs.'

'No, Martin, you won't.'

'How do you know?'

'You told me yourself – you said they reduce the risk of clots and strokes and stuff. Reduce the risk. So what's the worst thing that can happen?'

'I'll die of a stroke.'

'Realistically? No. You'll just be at a higher risk of having a stroke. That's if I'm wrong. And I'm not wrong.'

'A higher risk of having a stroke. You're OK with that?'

She takes a step closer. 'You're not going to have a stroke. None of it was true. There's nothing online about this condition. Nothing. I've checked. Your mam, she's just a GP, right? Shouldn't there be a specialist? Shouldn't there be regular check-ups and scans and tests and stuff? No, she does it all herself. Why? Because she can't let you be seen by another doctor because they'd know straight away that you're … like … from Krypton or something.'

'Krypton?'

'You know what I mean.'

Part of my brain can see the logic of this, but it's a very small part. The rest of it is screaming at me that I'm five minutes late for my meds. I haven't missed a set since I first began taking them. That's what? Eight years? Nearly half of my life.

'So you're saying they're both liars, right? They've been lying to me all my life?'

She shrugs. 'Well, yeah.'

'Great, fantastic.'

'Well, what would you do if you were in their position?' she says. 'You're from Persephone or someplace, living in deep cover, next thing your toddler starts flying around the supermarket or, I don't know, he torches some other kid with his laser vision.'

There's aspirin in one of the kitchen cupboards, but I can't think where I'm going to get more Hydroxithon. *If that's even what it is*, my brain whispers.

'Why do you just do these things?' I say. 'Why couldn't you ask me first?'

She looks at me like I'm an idiot. 'Because you'd have stopped me.'

I don't want to have a row with her, not on top of everything else, but it just makes me crazy. She gives this impression that she's taking the bull by the horns and seizing the day and all that stuff, but she acts like the fall never happened. No, hang on. Really, she acts like Enda was always like this. Won't talk about him as he was. And point-blank refuses to play the card-matching game or do any of that therapeutic stuff they took us through at the rehab place.

I don't say any of this, but it's as if I have a screen in my forehead that only she can read.

'Don't start,' she says, holding up her hands.

I take a deep breath. 'All I want to say is that Enda –'

'He wanted to get you off those drugs.'

'No, he didn't.'

Her face is set. This is not a conversation she wants to have. 'He spent hours online looking up stuff about the disease you're supposed to have. He went on forums. He asked questions. Couldn't find anybody who had your version of PCV. Not one person.'

'So it's rare,' I say. 'I know it's rare, we all know it's rare. That's not –'

'It's not just rare, Martin, it's not just rare. It's non-existent. He bought journals, you know that? Medical journals, and spent ages deciphering them. You remember the time he fell asleep in geography? He was up all night with a medical dictionary and some article about that allegedly mutated gene of yours. The whole night trying to figure it out. Why? Because your mother couldn't explain it.'

I remember that. I remember that day. Mr Cullen, the teacher, his voice is this nasal monotone, and he's got a thing about not opening windows. So it was hot and stuffy. Enda, he was sitting beside me with his head in his hands, and next thing he starts snoring. I went into a fake coughing fit to try and cover it and wake him up at the same time.

And he did plague my mother with questions. Sitting at the kitchen table, he'd straighten the glasses on his nose with the back of his hand, the way he used to, and he'd say, 'So, Helen, can I talk to you about the mutation in the gene JAK2. I know it produces a protein called tyrosine kinase. But can you explain again how it impacts the cytokine receptor signalling pathways?'

Mam loved it – at the start anyway. She would give me this sort of soppy grin that said, *It's so touching that your friend cares.* She would drop everything and sit down with him and explain terms and draw diagrams. Tina hadn't the patience for it. She'd roll her eyes and take out her phone. And to be honest, I didn't really care either. I mean, I knew I had this condition, but as long as I kept taking the pills, it didn't matter. I don't like taking them, but if they keep me alive, then fine, I'll take them. I mean, it would never have occurred to me that … that what? That I didn't need them? That they had been giving me them for some other reason?

'He made an appointment with some doctor,' says Tina, 'some ologist in America. A guy in a super-fancy hospital in New York. He persuaded him to do a video call with him. It was supposed to happen the week after the fall.'

'What? Why?'

'I told you. He knew it wasn't real. He said that, one, there were hardly any other cases out there where someone your age had it. Two, there were zero, *zero* cases where there were no symptoms.'

The room goes quiet.

'Why didn't he say any of this to me?'

She looks away now, and I can see that whatever she's remembering isn't something she wants to remember. 'He was going to. He just didn't get the chance.'

4. TRACTOR

We drop Enda home.

'You guys have a good day?' his mother asks.

'Yeah,' says Tina, shrugging.

I nod dumbly.

I have to remind Tina to text her mother to let her know she's staying in my house again tonight. Mrs O'Reilly is the opposite of my mother. Tina's brothers were all a bit wild, so as long as Tina doesn't steal or set fire to anything, she can pretty much do what she wants. I'm a battery kid, she's free-range.

I divide the night between staring at my phone and fretting over the fact that I'm off my meds. Again and again, I pull up Mam's last message.

> *When you're loading the dishwasher, make sure to turn the knives DOWN in case anyone stumbles onto them. Don't roll your eyes. This has happened!!! See you at lunchtime xxxooxx – 9:47am yesterday.*

When I try to sleep, the day's events pile up in my head like aeroplanes circling and circling with no place to land.

At 6.30, I'm wide awake again, wondering if my sick stomach is because of the no meds or the lack of sleep or the anxiety. I get up and wander silently around the house, ending up sitting on the swivel chair in the office downstairs. When I was younger, this used to be the play-room. The three of us – me, Tina and Enda – had dozens of sleepovers here. This is where we did most of our planning and playing and scheming.

One time, Enda decided we all needed to make wills. We were nine or something. We spent a couple of hours deciding who would get what if one of us got squished by an oil tanker or disappeared down a mineshaft. All I remember is that I was going to get Enda's microscope and Tina's remote-control Jag.

When my phone beeps just after seven, I jump. It's Sorcha, the woman who does secretarial work for Dad.

> *Hi Martin. Sorry I'm so late getting back to you. Usually leave phone off at weekends. Your dad said he was going to drop into his office on the way home. Everything OK?*

***

'Oh, it was super fab, Tina,' says Holly. 'You have got to go some time. We got a guy to take us on a boat through the mangrove forest and we saw deer and wild boar and river dolphins. And there was a tiger.'

'Babes, there was no tiger.'

'I saw him, Bills, I'm sure it was a tiger. And they're –'

'Babes, no way a tiger would let himself be seen in broad daylight.'

Holly ignores him. 'They're trying to build this power plant right on the river, just up from the forest. But wow!' She lays a hand on Tina's arm. 'There's this amazing group of activists, they keep sabotaging the site.' We're in Billy and Holly's camper van on the way out to Dad's office. Cycling there would take too long, and there's no-one else we can ask for a lift. We told them that my parents were away and that I needed to collect something.

Holly's driving. Tina's up beside her in the passenger seat. Billy and Enda are squished into the little seats either side of the table and Billy is laying out the cards in front of him. These are like playing cards, but with pictures instead of the usual hearts and clubs and all that. Just objects: a lamp, a spaceship, a car. Two of each in the deck. You lay them face down on the table. Turn over one, turn it back again. Then, when you turn over its mate, you try to remember where you saw the first one. If you find it on your go, you remove both from the table. And so on. The rehab people said it would stimulate his brain and help him recover. But Enda doesn't seem to get how it works, or at least, he's never managed to match a pair.

I'm watching Billy and Enda from the bench at the back of the van, trying to forget that I haven't taken my meds since yesterday afternoon. Billy treats Enda as if he's made out of glass, or matchsticks, like the smallest breeze could blow him apart. Billy's movements are small and careful and he talks so gently.

'OK, I'm going to turn over a card and you gotta remember where it is, yeah?' He looks at me to know if he's doing it right, and I nod. He turns over a card. Snake. Then he turns it back. Then another. Car. Then back again. The next three: a spatula, a boy, the other car.

Billy perks up expectantly but Enda doesn't go back for the first car. Instead, he turns over the boy again.

'No, man,' says Billy gently, 'the other car is ...'

Enda ignores him and goes for another card. Bird. Then a third.

'Banana.' I whisper this to myself. And when he turns it over, I'm right, it is the banana.

'Tina!' I call, but she's deep in conversation with Holly and doesn't hear me over the noise of the engine.

He did the same thing two days ago. The exact same thing. He turned over the same three cards in the same order: boy, bird, banana. That can't be a coincidence. It has to mean something. And just like the last time, Enda loses interest. His head drops and he stares at the floor. But before I can say anything more, Billy looks over at me, his hand goes across his mouth and his eyes glisten.

Oh God. I don't know what to do or where to look. He starts to say something, then stops, then starts again. In a whisper, so that he won't sob. He looks at Enda and says, 'I miss you, man.' And then he does sob. Twice. Two big silent sobs that make his body convulse. He's got his fists over his face now and he's holding his breath to try to stop it. I put my hand to my mouth and I clench my teeth so I won't crack.

'This is the turn, Martin, right?' Tina calls from the front seat. I can't answer her, so she looks back. 'Martin, this is it, yeah?'

I cough. 'Yeah.'

Billy wipes his face with the backs of his hands. 'This must be hell for you.'

I nod, staring at the floor.

It's years since I've been to Dad's office. It's in this beat-up little industrial estate with chain-link fences and bad roads and empty sites choked with weeds. There are warehouses with huge shutters, all of which are down and most of which are covered in bad graffiti. It's Sunday and the place is deserted. We rumble and bounce slowly through the potholes while I peer out, trying to remember which of the buildings is his. Holly is humming to herself, which sounds odd and out of place because the atmosphere is kind of edgy and sombre. I've been massaging the keys for the last ten minutes. There's always a spare set on the little rack in the kitchen, neatly labelled in Dad's square handwriting: 'Office'.

'That's it.'

A smallish house-like building surrounded by prefabs. Tina snort laughs. 'Hah! Could have spotted it a mile off.'

It's painted bright yellow with snow-white window-sills. No graffiti, no moss, no chipping paint.

Holly had spotted some flowers in one of the derelict sites we passed. She and Billy wander back that way, while Enda follows me and Tina to the front door, and in through the darkened corridor to his office. A sign on the door reads 'David Ryan – Consulting Engineer'. This room is in darkness too; you can just see the bulk of the desk from the light filtering in round the edges of the blind. I go over, pull it up and the room is flooded with light. Tina laughs. The opposite wall is awash with colour.

Pictures, floor to ceiling. Childish art. My childish art. Pictures I drew and painted and stuck together. Collages with dried pasta and googly eyes and fur and all sorts of things. Years and years of birthday and Christmas and Father's Day presents, completely covering the wall.

'Gosh.'

'You used to draw an awful lot of tractors, didn't you?'

I nod. 'I like tractors.'

'That one there has wings.'

Dad was never too busy. Never. No matter what he was doing, if I brought him a picture, he'd stop and sit down and get me to talk him through it.

'Now, they're wings, aren't they?'

'Yup.'

'And what's that thing at the back? Is it a fertiliser spreader?'

'No, it's a cloud sucker-upper.'

'Ah! Brilliant! You fly up there and you vacuum up all the clouds, right?'

'Yup.'

'That is a very good idea.' He nodded slowly, not smiling. He never told me I was brilliant at painting or that I would be a great artist or anything like that. But he took all my ideas dead seriously.

'What are you going to do with this one?' He held up the picture of the winged tractor reverentially.

'You can have it if you want.'

'Can I? Are you sure?'

'Yup.'

'Well, great. Thank you. I'll put it up in my office. If you need it back, let me know and I'll bring it home. I'm going to go and put it in the car so I won't forget it.'

And he'd kept them all, every single picture. I can't even remember half of them. Leaning in, I see that he's even dated them. In tiny handwriting, in black ink, at the bottom right-hand corner of each one. I reach out and touch the nearest one. Dated eight years earlier. A tractor with a plough, barely visible against the dark brown paint I used for the field. There's a pale blue sky crammed with 'M's of all shapes and sizes: seagulls. The paper is brittle and powdery to the touch.

Where are you, Dad? Where are you?

I turn to see Tina watching me. 'We'll find them,' she says quietly.

I nod. What else can I do?

Apart from the artwork, the office is like every other office in the world. Desk with a printer on a pedestal

41

alongside. Shelves lined with books, three fat grey filing cabinets: all locked. No computer, but that's not surprising. He takes his laptop everywhere. The desk is as empty as I'd expect Dad's desk to be. The drawers are full of stationery and the files he's working on. I flick through these but find nothing that strikes me as even vaguely relevant. I was hoping for a diary with details of where the seminar was on, but there's no sign of anything like that.

There's something on the floor. I can see the edge of it sticking out from under the desk.

It's his phone. The second I recognise it, it's like teetering on the edge of a pit that wasn't there a second ago.

'Is that his?'

I nod. It's dead. I look at Tina. I can see her struggling to think of something reassuring to say, but she just opens and closes her mouth.

'There's a spare charger at home,' I hear myself saying. 'We can charge it up and, I don't know ...'

Outside, we hear the rumble of Billy's voice. It sounds so far away, like it's reaching us from a distant galaxy.

'Let's just tell them, Martin. Billy and Holly. Let's just tell them that they're missing, that's all. Nothing else. We need help.'

'OK. Just that they're missing, though. Nothing else.'

Ten minutes later, we're sitting on the step of the van and Billy's trying to convince us that my parents have been abducted by aliens.

'Think about it, Martin, think about it.' He's got his arms spread wide, and his eyes are big and bright. 'It's exactly eighteen years ago since they first visited. Now they're back, to the exact same place, at the exact same time, and this time they're taking prisoners.'

We'd always kind of ignored the fact that Billy was a spacer, that the whole reason he comes here is to commemorate a UFO sighting. He was so great, he was so much fun that it wasn't hard to forget that he was also slightly daft. But of course he isn't daft at all. All those oddballs and weirdos who swarm into Glencooper every year, they're not oddballs and weirdos at all. They're right. There is life out there. It's the rest of us, the ones who rolled our eyes and made smart comments and laughed at them behind their backs, we're the idiots.

I look sideways at Tina and I can see she's only dying to tell him what we know. She glances at me and I give her the tiniest shake of my head. This frustrates her but I know she's not going to say anything.

'Can you just take us home, Holly?'

The whole way back to my house, Billy's going on and on about other abductions he's heard about and other UFO sightings. I try to zone out by doing the card game with Enda. Through all of this, he hasn't moved from his seat at the little table, and for the first time ever, he gets one right. I turn over the snake, and I'm about to turn it back down again, but he catches my hand and stops me. Then his hand hovers shakily over the table and falls on a card. I can tell he wants to flip it over, but he's tired and he can't get his fingers to do what he wants them to do, so I turn it over and it's the other snake. Two snakes. He actually matched a pair.

'Yes! Nice one, Enda! Tina! See this?' She's so wrapped up in what Billy is saying that I have to call her a second time. 'See? A match. He did that.'

Tina nods distractedly and turns back to Billy. 'That's class, Enda, well done.'

I keep going. I turn over the lamp and turn it back, then the train, then turn it back. Then the ladybird, then the other lamp. I pause, waiting to see if he can remember where the first lamp is. His hand rises and moves unsteadily over the cards.

'Yeah, that's it, dude,' I tell him. 'You can do this. Tina, look!'

'Just a sec.' She doesn't even look over.

I bite back my annoyance and focus on Enda. This time his hand doesn't fall on the first lamp. He lurches forward and reaches again for the two snakes, which I've removed from the game and left to one side. He tries to pick them up but they slide beneath his groping fingers and flutter to the ground. I stoop, grab them and replace them on the table. He reaches for them again.

OK, right, that's not the game, but what he's doing, it feels … intentional.

'What is it, Enda?' I lean forward, trying to move into his eye line, but he's exhausted by all this and he just slumps back into the seat.

Holly drops us to my house, and as I open the front door, Tina is all about what Billy's been saying. Aliens and abductions and conspiracies. I ignore her and keep going into the kitchen, where I dig out a spare charger and plug Dad's phone in. It's completely dead and won't power up right away.

'What?' she says.

'What do you mean, "What"?'

She's standing in the kitchen doorway, hands on hips. 'You're all mad about something.'

'Yeah, I'm mad. I'm fed up of the fact that you make no effort. I mean, the least you could do is acknowledge it when something goes well.'

She rolls her eyes. 'Oh, this again.'

'He's never done that before. He's never matched a pair. It's progress, Tina. It's good news.'

'Is there any food?' She walks past me and starts opening cupboards.

'Seriously. Food?'

'I'm hungry.'

'I don't understand why –'

She slams a cupboard door closed. 'Things are the way they are, OK?' she says. 'Enda is the way he is. Stop making out that he's …' She's looking around for the right word but can't find it. 'Stop making out that he's getting better, OK? Just stop.'

'He matched two cards, for the first time, and then –'

'Look at him.' She grabs my elbow and drags me to

the kitchen window. He's outside, standing by the shed, gazing at the ground. 'That's it,' she says. 'That's all we've got. OK?'

'They said that –'

'They said that he might get a tiny bit better, Martin. So, yeah, OK, maybe he did match a couple of cards. Fine.' She throws open her arms. 'So what? What good is that to me?'

'What good is that *to you?*'

'You know what I mean.'

There's no point in saying any more. I sit there staring at the big battery icon on Dad's phone, waiting for it to charge enough so I can turn it on. Tina finds bread and puts it in the toaster. Through the window, I see Enda push the door of the shed and disappear inside.

I've just managed to wake Dad's phone up – his passcode is my birthday– when she comes over and places a plate with two slices of buttered toast in front of me.

'Thanks.'

'Find anything?'

I flick through his email and his message apps and find a draft text. To me. Written at 7.14 yesterday morning. Never sent. It says *Sing .;7*. That's all. *Sing .;7*. We both stare at it.

'He pocket-dialled it,' says Tina.

Again, I have that same sensation – that I'm standing on the edge of an abyss, about to pitch forward into it.

Sing .;7 Sing .;7 Sing .;7

There's something about that. Maybe he didn't pock-et-dial, maybe he was rushing, maybe he –

And then I get it.

'Signal 87,' I say. 'Signal 87.'

5. SIGNAL

Tina brings toast out to Enda while I go upstairs to my parents' bedroom. The air is cool, the room perfectly neat. There's not a crease on the bedspread; the sheet is folded down like in a hotel. Mam said she learned how to do this when she worked as a chambermaid in a hotel in Greece when she was in college. Is that true? Did that really happen?

I open the wardrobe and see the flat wooden box that my father made sitting on the high shelf, the words 'Signal 87' stencilled along the side. Before I pull out a chair to get up to it, I can't resist the urge to push my face into my mother's dangling clothes and smell her smell. It's a mistake, because I have to fight to stop myself crying again. I take the box into my room for a minute to pull myself together.

Signal 87 is a board game that Dad invented. It's got dice, forfeit and bonus cards and a long list of rules on a folded A3 sheet. The object of the game is this: get to the top of the mountain and send a distress signal before the enemy force invades. I know it's just a game, but the thing is, Dad only ever takes it out on Christmas Day. And when he's tidying it up and putting it away, he always says, 'You can play this when your mother and I are gone.' Every time.

Without fail. I always thought it was a bit morbid, especially at Christmas, but was he trying to tell me something?

I bring the box downstairs to Tina, place it on the table and lift off the top. I expect to see the little matchbox with counters in it, the dice, the cards and folded board, but I don't see any of these things. Instead, there's a white envelope with my name on it. This is sitting on top of a sleek white plastic box with thin black lines running along the side. Tina takes this out while I tear open the envelope. Inside, there's a letter in my father's handwriting.

This is what it says.

> *My dear child, our wonderful boy, Martin,*
>
> *If you are reading this, we are not there. I will get straight to the point. You need to send the signal. Just like we talked about. Send the signal. You must act quickly, Martin. I can't stress this enough. The instructions are on the other side of this page. Once you have read this, take the box, leave the house and don't come back. Stay with Tina or Enda. All will be well, I promise you.*
>
> *We love you and we think the world of you.*
> *Dad*

'"Just like we talked about"? "Just like we talked about"?' I hold the letter in front of my face and shout at it. 'We didn't bloody talk about it, did we? You kept it all to yourselves!'

But behind the anger, there's this rising nausea. It's like a siren is going off in my head. It's real. It's real. It's real. It's real. It's real. It's real. They're actual aliens. They're not from here. Earth, like. For the last however many hours I've been expecting them to show up. I've been expecting them to jump out from behind the couch or something and yell 'Surprise! Gotcha!' I was sure, deep down, that it had to be some kind of prank, that there had to be some sort of reasonable explanation, but there isn't. I can't fool myself any more. It's real. He actually did fly; he did actually make those leaves fly. And, and … they're missing. They're actually really missing. This isn't about a lost phone or a puncture or even a car crash. They're missing, and … they're aliens. They're honest-to-God, real-life aliens. These two people that I love so much, that I can't live without.

Tina's read the letter. '"Send the signal",' she says. 'Who to? Why?'

I'm walking back and forth in the kitchen. 'I don't know, I don't know, I don't know.'

She checks the wooden box again, but there's nothing else in there.

'They were going to tell me, obviously. They just …' I feel all of the anger slosh out of me. They were on the point of telling me. Only now something bad – maybe something really bad – has happened.

The white plastic box with the black lines is small and light and isn't much bigger than a pencil case. It doesn't appear to have any controls. No buttons, no dials, no touch screen. The instructions on the reverse of the letter are infuriatingly perfect. There isn't a single crossing-out. Each line is slightly indented, each instruction numbered. I read and reread it.

Keep moving, I think to myself. If I keep moving, keep doing things, I won't have to think. Thinking's the enemy. Thinking's the thing that'll make me throw up or have a panic attack or throw up while having a panic attack.

'We're to take it up to Garrenturk,' I say. 'He's installed something in the base of the old engine-room chimney. This thing'll work automatically when we're there. Come on.'

But she's just sitting there. There's half a slice of toast left on her plate.

'Tina?'

'Yeah, coming.'

They planned to tell me, they must have. The letter assumes I know so much more than I know. If it didn't, there would be much more detail: who I am, who they are, where we come from, what they're doing here, who I'm signalling to. *You need to send the signal. Just like we talked about* … in that long conversation that we were going to have but never got around to. I'm fifteen next month. That's when they were going to sit me down.

Right?

The whole way down through the village and up to Garrenturk, I'm going back and forth over the last few months like a guy with a metal detector who knows he dropped his keys around here somewhere. Was there a moment last Christmas, as she was putting the game away? We were all on the rug in front of the fire. Mam was gathering up the cards and shuffling the edges together on the hearth. I was picking up the pieces and putting them in the matchbox. Dad was sitting on the floor, his back to the couch. And he said her name. He said 'Helen' in such a peculiar, serious way that we both stopped and looked up.

I looked from one to the other. He had the strangest look on his face, like he was trying to keep it completely expressionless, but at the same time his eyes were, like, dialled up to eleven on the intensity scale.

She must have signalled to him. A jerk of her head or something, because next thing they both stood up.

'What?' I said. 'What's going on?'

'We just need a minute, Martin,' she said.

They left the room and were gone for five minutes. When they came back, Mam's face was red, Dad was sullen, and the temperature had dropped by ten degrees. They wouldn't tell me what it was about.

'Grown-up stuff. Between me and your dad' was all she'd say.

And there was this tension between them for the rest of the day. They tried to pretend there wasn't, but with us, it takes ages for the ripples to die away. We were watching some film and I caught him, several times, looking over at her, his face half puzzled, half annoyed. And she wasn't really taking anything in. She spent more time looking at the fire than the screen.

I just figured it was a row. They don't have many of them, but they do have them.

He wanted to tell me – that was it. He thought that the moment had come, but she didn't. She wanted to wait.

* * *

The ruins of the engine room that powered the lifts and trolleys in the old mines stand on a low hill overlooking the Atlantic at Garrenturk, not far from the village. There are broken-down stone houses and a tall, dismal-looking chimney. The whole thing is surrounded by security fences and keep-out signs, but the fence is more dilapidated than the ruins and is full of holes. We dump the bikes and start to climb towards the cluster of buildings, but as soon as we do, I stop. Voices, over by the engine room.

'You hear that?'

Tina rolls her eyes. 'It's Benny Doyle.'

Benny Doyle. Glencooper's only home-grown spacer. He does walking tours of the village, following the route that the UFO was supposed to have taken and selling people overpriced T-shirts with pictures of spaceships on them. He's also a ghostbuster in his spare time. He wears this denim jacket with writing on the back: 'Need an Exorcist? Call Benny.' And it gives his phone number. This weekend is the highlight of his year.

When we get up to the buildings, there are at least six people crowding around him, and he's got a microphone hooked up to a speaker dangling around his chest.

'From here, the craft progressed in an easterly direction and was seen on this very spot by fourteen-year-old Olive Doyle, who was on her way to the village to pick up a bottle of milk for her mother. Olive, who is my second cousin, is now working in Manchester as a nutritionist.'

Tina and I loiter by the bikes while Enda wanders up the hill. Eventually, Benny stops talking and we see him turn and lead the little group of tourists down the hill.

The chimney is tall. Standing at the base and looking up, it feels like it's falling away from us, but it's just the clouds moving in the background.

There's a noise from my backpack. We both hear it and look at each other. It's not a beeping, mechanical noise, more a kind of chirrup. I shrug off the backpack, swing it round and carefully take out the box. There's now a band of green light running across the top. I hand the thing to Tina and pull my father's instructions from my pocket.

'You need to place it on the ground near the base of the chimney,' I say. 'He installed an antenna on the inside of the chimney, and it should be able to connect automatically.'

She stoops and places the thing on the mossy concrete. The green light changes suddenly to purple, exactly as the instructions said it would.

'We've just got to wait now. It'll turn red when it starts broadcasting.'

I'm staring at it, waiting, but it's still purple when Tina steps up, raises her foot and brings her boot crashing down on the machine. The green light dies instantly. Before I can cry out or push her away, she stomps on it again and it gets flipped into the air and lands with a hollow tinkling sound on the concrete.

I dive on it before she can do any more damage. 'Tina, what are you doing? What's wrong with you?'

The green light is gone. The top is dented, and when I pick it up, something inside rattles. Breathing heavily, I place it back at the base of the chimney, crouching over it protectively, but it's dead. There's no light, no sound, nothing. Dead.

'Martin, I'm really sorry. I had to do that.'

I'm nearly in tears. 'That was my only chance to get them back, Tina, my only chance.'

'They're not what you think, Martin. They're sleepers, Martin. Spies.'

'What are you on about?'

She holds up her hands. 'I'm not saying you're one of the bad guys, OK, but think about it, Martin. We discover their secret, and next thing they disappear.'

My whole body has gone limp. I feel like I'm made of nothing.

'This isn't a distress signal, Martin. What does the letter say? "You need to send the signal." To do what? We don't know. But it's not something good, Martin, it can't be. Martin. Martin, listen.' She gets down on the ground beside me, where I'm crouching with the dead white box. 'They're not the good guys. I just know they're not. I just know.'

She puts her hand on my shoulder, but I slap it away and stand up. 'How could you just know? They're my parents. You think you know them better than I do?'

She gets to her feet slowly.

'Do you?' I repeat.

'I heard them talking, Martin. Last year, after the fall. Remember the time I forgot my hat? It was December; we'd been doing that science project on the planets. Remember? You waited on the road and I went back to your house to get it.'

I can't even look at her.

'I was gone ages, remember? I overheard them talking, Martin. I called out when I came in. I said, "Only me!" but they never heard me. So I went up to your room and next thing they were out on the landing, just outside your door. I think they must have been in their bedroom. I was about to come out, but then I realised they were arguing, arguing in these really low voices. It was weird.'

Now I know that something horrible is coming. It's like a tidal wave surging towards me, and all I can do is stand helpless on the beach. That is how they argue. That's exactly how they argue. In whispers, standing close together, like they're in a church or a library or somewhere public. I thought all couples argued like this, but they don't, of course they don't.

'I didn't want to eavesdrop, so I was about to cough or something, but before I could, they were in the thick of it and I was too embarrassed to admit I'd heard them. Your dad, Martin, he wanted to reduce your meds. He said that there was no need for five doses a day, he said it wasn't ... he said you only needed one. He used words I didn't understand, and don't remember now, but he never mentioned polywhatsitsname, not once. He never mentioned blood or clots or strokes or anything like that. But your mother objected. She said, "We can't reduce them. If we do that without telling him why, he'll suspect something."'

I look up at her for the first time.

'That's why I've been watching you like a hawk for the past six months. That's the real reason I dumped your meds yesterday. You think for a moment I would have done that if I thought I was putting you in danger? I didn't want to tell you because ... I know you love them, Martin, of course you do, they're your parents, but ... but I don't think they are who you think they are. I think they've been drugging you for years, and, and I think they're sleepers. Spies. Sent here to ... I don't know, figure us out or something.'

I get up, put the box back into my bag and head for the bikes.

'Martin, why do you think they kept you in the dark? Because they knew you wouldn't be able to accept the truth. And the truth is that they're the enemy. They've been working against us the whole time.'

'You've doomed us,' I say, pulling my bike up out of the heather. 'You've doomed us. Spies? They're not spies. That's just some crap Billy made up. They've been ...

they've been taken by, I don't know, something bad, and we were supposed to send a distress signal.'

'We don't know that, Martin.'

'Yes we do, yes we do. That's why they dragged that game out once a year. They couldn't tell me the full truth, cos it's so mind-blowing, but they made sure I would know what to do when the time came. They were calling for backup.'

'Well, we agree on *that*,' says Tina

And I'm about to cycle off, but I don't. Instead, I drop the bike again. I know what I'm going to say and I can't wait to say it. I just so desperately need to wound her. 'You've ruined everything, just like when Enda fell.'

'What?'

'Tell the truth, Tina. Where did you go?'

'What has this got to do with –?'

'You ran away. I know you did.'

'Martin, I –'

'I climbed down that cliff and knelt there with his head on my knees and my hand down his throat, trying to keep his airway open, because when I called 999, that's what the guy said to do. And the whole time, I was calling out to you, but you were gone. You ran away.'

'I was getting help!'

'You ran away, Tina. I was down there for fifty-seven minutes. There was blood gurgling up out of his throat and I was trying to do what the paramedic was telling me, but I was afraid I was choking him or letting him choke or something, and there was blood everywhere. And at the same time, I was trying to explain to the guy exactly where we were. And I kept thinking, *OK, she'll take twelve minutes to get to the village and tell someone; then it won't be any more than five minutes before she'll be back up in someone's car.* But then it was twenty minutes, then twenty-five, then thirty, then forty then fifty. No, Tina. You know what that was like? I thought he was dying. You left me. You left us. I know you did.'

She's been standing there, jaw clenched, listening to me, her face getting harder and harder. I want to make her cry but she's just mad. Really, really mad. She rushes past me, picks up her bike and takes off.

'Run away again, Tina.'

She drops the bike and comes back and I think she's going to punch me or something, but she just says, 'I was getting help.' Then she turns and picks up her bike again. In half a minute, she's a dot on the road, pedalling madly down the hill.

Enda, who's been hovering there in the background the whole time, now walks past me, picks up his bike and takes off after her.

6. DARKNESS

Last year, not long after the fall, when Enda was still in the rehabilitation place in Dublin, I started to get these … I don't know what to call them. Anxiety attacks? I stopped sleeping and used to get up in the middle of the night to check the back door was locked. And then, after I convinced myself that it was, I'd go back upstairs and lie there, staring at the ceiling and worrying about whether or not the windows were closed or the gas was left on or the smoke alarms were working. I'd been at this for weeks before Dad came down one night and found me pouring water on the ashes in the grate, just to make sure the fire was out.

He said that anxiety was like a hungry beast, and that the more you fed it, the more it would want. 'You can never satisfy it, Martin, no matter how many times you get up to lock the door or check the switches are off or whatever it is. Your anxiety will always come up with some new threat that you have to go and fix.'

My father has three pairs of flannel pyjamas, which he changes every two to three days. Blue for Monday and Tuesday, red for Wednesday and Thursday, green for Friday to Sunday. It must have been the weekend because he was dressed in green.

'You've got to think of it like …' Dad was always a storyteller. Hang on, stop, stop. Not was. *Is*. When I was younger, he was the one who came up with complicated tales of fabulous beasts and terrible battles and evil wizards. He used to tell me long, rambling stories at nighttime. Quest stories that went on for weeks.

'Anxiety is like a smelly person on the bus.'

'I thought it was like a hungry beast.'

'No, smelly person on the bus is better. So, right, you're sitting on the bus and this Mr Stinky gets on and he sits down next to you and the smell is awful. He hasn't washed or shaved in weeks and you can see bits of egg and beans in his beard, and his clothes are wet and matted in filth. You get the idea. But every time you get up and change seats, he gets up and follows you around.'

'So I get off the bus. Walking's better for you anyway.'

'No, no, you can't get off the bus. You have to stay on the bus.'

'Why? That's awful. So what am I supposed to do?'

'You don't get up – you sit beside him and get used to the stink.'

'But –'

'It'll be awful for a while, but in time you'll get used to it, and then, eventually, you just won't smell it any more.'

'You need to work on your material, Dad.'

'Yeah, but you get the idea, right?' He raised his eyebrows and I nodded.

'Get used to the stink,' I said, 'because it's not going anywhere.'

'And after a while, you won't notice it at all. Really, honestly, it's true.'

Where are they? Where? What happened to them? What if they're …? I mean, what if they're …? I can't say the word, can't think it.

In the letter, Dad said, 'All will be well, I promise you.' He's never broken a promise. Never. But then it looks like they've been lying to me all my life.

I can't believe they're bad people. I just can't. I mean, they love Mam round here. People show up at the house at all hours of the day and night, with falls and fevers and things, and she never, ever sends them away and never, ever complains. She gets people coming up to her all the time, and they shake her hand and say things like, 'I can never repay you, Dr Ryan, for what you did.' A couple of months ago, we were in town, and we met a woman pushing a buggy with another kid running after her and she says to me, 'See that little lad there, if it wasn't for your ma, he wouldn't be here. She's a miracle worker, your ma.'

But I also believe Tina. *He'll suspect something.* That's what she heard my mother say. And it's been twenty-four hours since my last set of meds and I'm not sick. Well, I am sick, but it's all exhaustion and anxiety and anger and terror. At least I think it is.

'OK,' I say aloud, 'let's assume they're evil.'

That means that the signal I tried to send this morning was designed to do something bad like, I don't know, summon an army of mutant killer insects or something. So by not sending that signal, did we stop an attack? Or slow it down? If so, great.

But what if they're not evil, Mam and Dad? What if they're here to do something good? Or prevent something bad? The signal was supposed to be a call for help. But because of Tina there's no help coming. Which means I'm the only one who can do anything.

Me.

I feel like I'm sitting on a bus full of stinky people, and we're speeding down a mountain road and the brakes don't work.

* * *

Two days ago, when we were putting up the trail cams, I was quivering like a leaf halfway up a tree. The worst that could have happened if I fell was a sprained ankle. Now, I'm so far down the mineshaft that I can't see the opening any more and I have no idea how much further I have to go. If I fall, I'm dead, dead squared. I'm clinging to this ladder like grim death, but I really have no idea if I can trust it. So many flakes of rust stick to my sweaty hands, it's like they're coated in sand. And it's so dark, I can't tell if my eyes are open or closed. Down I go. Down and down and down, breathing in and out slowly, trying not to think about how far I could fall.

I spent ages going through emails and messages and files on Dad's phone, but all I could find was work stuff. Construction projects going back years: specifications, plans, lists of materials, invoices, receipts. There was nothing out of the ordinary, nothing unconnected to work, except one thing. It was in one of his note-taking apps among shopping lists, reminders, films that people recommended to him and things like that.

Two columns. The one on the left made up of strings of letters and numbers. MS 1 (M), MS2 (K), MS 2.5 (Ir). The second column seemed to be dates – all from the last couple of weeks. There was something about this list that kept bringing me back to it. It just didn't seem to have anything to do with anything else that I'd seen. I stared and stared before it dawned on me. MS 1, MS 2. Mineshaft 1, Mineshaft 2. And the letters in brackets? (M) and (K) and so on? They must all stand for the names of the people who own the land where the shaft is. 'M' is for Maher's, 'K' is Kiely's. That's how people around here identify them.

It figures. I mean, why are my parents in Glencooper of all places? Before they arrived, the village was famous for one thing. The mines. For fifty years in the late 1800s, thousands of miners from all over Europe descended on the place and made Swiss cheese out of it. No matter where you go in Glencooper, you're walking over a network of tunnels that run deep underground. There are thirty-seven entrances to mineshafts in the twenty square kilometres between Garrenturk and the Knocknagown Woods. Some are completely filled in and concreted over. Most of the rest of them are flooded, but there's one that you can still get down into. It's in Maher's field, which is about three kilometres from my house.

So I cycle over and hide my bike in a little copse of trees in a corner of the field. When I pick my way over the grass, no-one stops me. No-one stops me when I duck under the fence surrounding the pit, past the 'Keep Out' and 'Danger: Open Shaft' signs. And no-one stops me when I lift aside the boards and climb down into the hole. The most surprising thing about it is that I don't stop myself. Most of my brain is screaming at me to turn back, to go home and hide under the bed.

And now, my foot reaches for the next rung and the next rung isn't there. For a second I think I'm going to fall. My other foot slips off and I dangle there in the darkness. Is this it? The bottom of the pit? It has to be, doesn't it? Why else would the ladder end? I try to dip my head to look down, but what's the point? This is more than darkness. It's big and black and cold and awful.

'Oh God.' My voice echoes in the darkness, like I'm at the bottom of an empty swimming pool.

Then I let go.

It's OK, I was right, I land on something solidish. Timber, but it's slippery and my feet almost go out from under me. I fall back against a damp, rocky wall, but don't quite fall. I just stand there, panting in the pitch darkness, hearing nothing but my own breathing echoing and the dripping of water into water somewhere ahead of me. I'm stiff from the climb, so it takes a minute to swing my backpack round. My hands are frozen – wish I'd thought of gloves – and covered in rust, so I wipe them on my T-shirt, then grope inside the backpack for my phone. This far beneath the ground, there's no signal, but that's OK. I never expected that there would be. I turn on the torch and see that I'm at the base of the pit all right, in a space slightly wider than the tunnel which leads away from it. I look up towards the lowest rungs of the ladder. Could I get up to them, I wonder? Could I jump and grab the lowest rung? Would I have the strength to pull myself up to the next?

'No,' I say aloud, 'not a smelly hope.'

I check the phone. Ninety-two per cent, but the torch will eat that up pretty quickly. Better get moving.

The tunnel is held up with these timber frames that march off into the darkness. The beams are fat and grey and look like they've been here since forever. The boards beneath my feet feel soft and damp. Ahead of me, I can see where they've started to rot away.

Very soon after I start off down the tunnel, I get this weird feeling down my left arm. Sort of numb and weak and pins-and-needlesy. I flex my fingers and rub my arm, thinking that it must be something to do with the climb down.

The light shows maybe three or four metres of tunnel ahead. The wall is rough and damp and rocky. It gets horribly narrow, then widens out again, then a huge ridge of stone sticks out from the side and I have to turn sideways and press myself against the opposite wall to get by. It's much colder than I expected, and the air is still – weirdly still. The only sound is echoing drips of water, behind and in front of me. I have a raincoat in my bag, so I lower the phone onto the damp boards and prop it there while I dig the coat out. Once I get it on, I spend half a minute massaging my shoulder, trying to get some feeling back into it. If this weakness doesn't pass, I won't be able to climb back up. Then I remember that I won't be able to reach up to the ladder in the first place.

So that's OK then.

I keep going, down and down. What am I looking for, exactly? What could Dad have been doing here? Assuming he ever actually came down here. If he wanted me to send a signal, then he's got – they've got – some kind of protective role, right? If that list did refer to the mineshafts, what was he doing with them? Keeping them clear of mutant alien insects? Sweeping for negative energy bombs?

An opening on my right appears, with another of those ancient frames at the entrance. I stoop and look into it. It looks just the same as this one. I decide to stick to the main tunnel for the time being. The long timbers which lined the base of the passage become more and more rotten the further I go, until they give out completely and then it's just mud and rock with more and bigger puddles of black water. I come on other passageways, branching off left and right, then longer puddles. I have to edge around them to keep my feet from getting wet. I'm shivering now; the raincoat is really thin and gives zero warmth. My fingers are so cold that it's hard to hold onto the phone. I try to switch hands, just to give my right hand a break, but it's a mistake. I drop the phone into the water.

Bang. Darkness.

'No!' I fall to my knees and rummage frantically in the freezing water. 'No!' Two seconds, three seconds. My hand closes on it and pulls it out, but it's dead, dead as mud, dead as rock.

It's over. I have to turn back. So I turn back.

I squelch along, one hand on the wall, the other out in front. There's something really wrong with my left arm now. I mean, I can barely lift it. I can still flex my fingers, but that's it.

I'm tense as a guitar string, afraid I'll accidentally turn down one of those side passages and end up wandering around in the darkness for the rest of my short life. No-one knows I'm here, and now that Tina hates me, there's nobody to notice I'm gone.

Then I see a light up ahead. It's very dim, but it's definitely there. I blink once, twice, just to prove to myself it's not a trick my eyes are playing on me. I stop dead and listen, but there's nothing to hear except the irregular drip of water and my own ragged breathing. If this is the enemy, if this is the mutant killer insects, well, there's not much I can do about it, is there? All I've got in my bag is a bottle of water, some rope, an apple and a salami sandwich. Then I see it. A small round something, glowing on the ground ahead. Glowing green. Weird. How could I have missed it on the way down?

'No, no, no no no!' The worst has happened. I've taken a wrong turn. That's it. I'm definitely dead now. *Hang on, no, wait.* I realise I'm back at the ridge of rock, the one sticking out into the middle of the passage, the one I had to edge around sideways to get past earlier. The glowing green thing is half buried in the mud in the corner behind this rock. The light from it is so dim that it would have been easy to miss it when the torch was working. It's warm to the touch. Round, but not quite spherical; smooth and glossy. It weighs, I don't know, a kilogram? It's not a lamp; it's not like anything I've seen before. Without thinking too hard about whether I should or not, I shake it. It doesn't rattle, and there's no smell from it either. Is this it? The negative energy bomb planted by the mutant killer insects, designed to blow the Earth to smithereens?

My left arm has gone so weak now that it's practically useless. It dangles there while I try to wrestle the green thing into my backpack. Then it hits me. This isn't some stiffness from the climb down. This is me off my meds for – what? Thirty hours now? My face feels funny. I try to move my jaw but it's hanging uselessly open and won't respond.

'I'm having a stroke.' That's what I try to say, but the words don't come out right. Oh God. I'm actually having a stroke. I'm fourteen years old and I'm having a stroke. And as I think that, I look back down the passage to where the green-glowing possible negative energy bomb has rolled and I blink because it looks like there are two of them, but there's not, there's only one. My vision is starting to go. It's a stroke. I know the symptoms. Mam drilled them into me. She drilled them into me. When I was six. Because it was a risk, even with the meds.

'How do you recognise a stroke, Martin?'

Sitting at the table, eating cornflakes. Morning sunshine streaming through the window. The back door open and Dad whistling in the garden.

'Weakness down one side, blurred vision, trouble talking, confusion.'

'And you'll tell me or Dad if you ever get any one of those, right?'

'Yeah.'

'Straight away, promise?'

'Yeah.'

How could I have doubted her? How could I?

I go back, scoop up the green ball and fumble it into my backpack. Then I stumble on up the passage, thinking about nothing now but the ladder. But it's no good. My left side doesn't feel like it's mine any more. Then my legs don't want to carry me and I slump down onto the damp boards and …

7. SPACERS

One minute I'm flying around the Brenner Stack – a tall column of rock that stands in the sea a little way out from the cliffs near Enda's house. Tina and my mother are there too. We're about to do something really important, but then I can't remember what, and then I begin to suspect I'm dreaming. The real world starts to elbow its way in. I can smell the sea and there's a breeze from somewhere. It feels like I'm neither outside nor inside. No pain. I'm not in pain. But then I haven't moved yet.

Wait a sec, wait a sec. I'm not dead.

This is a big surprise.

'Oh, hey, honey, you're awake!'

Holly's face is there suddenly. Short blond hair, tie-dyed bandana, huge blue eyes. She puts her hand on my arm and squeezes it.

'You OK, baby?' she asks softly. 'Can you talk? Does it hurt?'

I try to speak, but my mouth is dry.

'You need a drink?'

Next thing she's lifting my head and holding a cup up to my lips.

'Martin!' Cool Billy appears just behind her. 'What were you doing down there? Crazy place to take a nap.' He's in an orange vest that's a few sizes too small for him. I'm in their camper van, and the sliding door is pulled back.

'Did you hit your head or something, baby?' Holly's voice is like honey and maple syrup and treacle all mixed up together.

I had a stroke, right? I flex my arms, my legs, my jaw. I rub the side of my face. Everything seems to be working the way it should. 'How did you get me up?'

'Billy carried you up, baby,' she says, smoothing my hair back from my face.

'Really?' Billy's big and ripped, yes, but I was a long way down. I can't imagine how he managed to carry me all the way out.

It's like Holly reads my mind. 'He just slung you over his shoulder and flew up the ladder.'

This is super awkward. She's hovering over me like I'm an egg and she's some kind of fabulous bird.

'I should get up.' I push back the covers, sit up and pivot around. I feel fine. My vision is not blurry. I flex my fingers and feel no weakness. I should be paralysed. I should be unable to talk. So maybe it wasn't a stroke?

Suddenly, Tina's there in the doorway.

'You have Tina to thank for getting you out. She got Billy to look for you.'

'You OK?' she says.

I nod. 'How did you know where I was?'

She shrugs. *I just knew*, the shrug says.

Through the open door, I see Enda outside on the sand.

'She's good,' says Cool Billy, pointing double-handed at Tina. 'I thought it was a wild goose chase, but your friend here can be very persuasive.'

'Tina, can you try to call Mam and ...'

Her head is shaking before I finish. 'Tried them three times, both numbers. Nothing.'

What did I expect? That I'd wake up and everything would be fine? That Tina would smile and say that Mam was on her way? That Dad was waiting in the car park, that he had the most rational explanation I ever heard? At least she's talking to me. I seriously thought she'd never speak to me again.

Hang on, hang on, hang on. Something's weird.

They're looking at me. Holly and Billy are looking at me like I'm ... Oh, I get it. Tina's told them. She's told them everything.

'So!' Billy claps his hands together. 'I hear you're not from around here.'

When I look at Tina, she shrugs again. 'We need help, Martin,' she says.

'She's told you about Mam and Dad?'

'Yeah, dude, that's heavy,' says Billy.

I look up at him. 'Have you got any theories? Any ideas about where they might be?'

'That's a big question.' He folds his arms and furrows his brow. 'You got any idea what they were doing here in the first place?'

'Did Tina tell you about the signal?'

He nods.

I clear my throat. 'I think they had a job here. I think they were trying to do something, something important.' I avoid looking at Tina as I say this. 'I think something bad is going to happen. I think they were supposed to stop it, or to warn someone that it was going to happen. I think they were taken by someone who didn't want that signal to go out.'

'Dude.' Billy gets down on his hunkers. 'That's heavy.'

Holly puts a hand on my arm. 'We'll help you any way we can, honey, you know that. Would you like a soda?' She stands up and goes to the fridge.

The strangest silence settles on the place. It's weird. It's like everyone has suddenly lost the power of speech. I look out through the door and there's Enda, staring straight at me again. I'm starting to realise something. Something big. Then it's gone again. It's like trying to remember a dream just after you've woken up, feeling it break apart and disappear as you reach for it. Something important has happened, and some part of my brain knows that, but I can't quite …

'You OK?' It's Tina.

'Enda,' I say, and Tina turns and sees him staring straight at me. This shocks her. I can see it in the way her body tenses. She turns back and looks at me with a quizzical expression.

'That's the second time he's done that,' I tell her.

Holly pops a can, leans back against the little counter and sips. Billy is still squatting there with a frown on his face.

Silence.

I have this sense of overwhelming wrongness. Like, I don't know, someone's been messing with reality.

'Two snakes.' I blurt out the words. Everyone looks at me. 'Two snakes.'

Tina says, 'What is it, Martin?'

'Enda turned over two snakes.'

'So?' Tina says it, but it's not a challenge. It's like she's felt it too, the weirdness.

Enda's still staring at me. 'The cards. He turned over two snakes. He was trying to tell us something.'

No-one says anything. Tina's looking hard at me.

'Two snakes.' I look up at Billy and Holly, then pull over my bag and reach in. 'You know what this is, don't you?'

I draw out the green thing. The second it sees the light of day, Holly spits out her drink, pushes past Billy, tears open one of the cupboards and pulls out something small and dark. Next thing she kicks the green ball from my hands. It lands on the bed, and before I can say or do anything, she shoves me out of the way and aims two-handed at it. A beam of blue light shoots from the dark something in her hand and rakes the green ball. For the shortest moment, it seems transparent. I see something curled up inside it. I see it pulsate, then go still. The blue light is sucked back into the thing that Holly is holding, and the dim green light from the ball dies.

It's like someone has hit me with a freeze ray; it's like I've suddenly forgotten how to breathe.

Holly puts the blue-light thing on a shelf, then turns around and looks at me coldly. Coldly? That doesn't do it justice. It's not a look I've seen before, not on anyone in real life. It's hatred and disgust and maybe even fear. And it tells me something that I don't believe and that I'm sure of at the same time. Holly isn't Holly. She's not who we thought she was. She pulls the bandana from her head, as if it's part of a disguise that there's no point in wearing any more. Then she uses it to wrap up the green thing, except it's not green any more – it looks … dead. Which means that up to a few moments ago, it wasn't dead.

'Who are you?' I don't decide to say this, but it's what comes out.

Billy giggles. He actually giggles. He's squatting there with a hand over his mouth trying to cover a nervous grin.

'Who are you?' I say it again. I can't think of anything else to say.

Holly turns to me. 'Who am I?' She raises her eyebrows. 'I'm the one who saves the planet, that's who I am.'

Even her accent is different. It was fake, it was all fake.

'Was that an egg?' says Tina. 'That was an egg, wasn't it?'

Holly doesn't answer. She takes the egg – if that's what it is – to the front of the camper and does something with it, something we can't see.

'What's going on?' Tina almost shouts it.

Through all of this, Billy's been squatting there smothering that same nervous laugh.

'Babes?' he says tentatively, but Holly ignores him too, so he turns to us.

'Well, guys,' he says, 'Martin here isn't the only one who's not, well, local.'

'You're aliens,' I say.

'Guilty as charged!' says Billy. 'Well, not really – I mean, we're human, we're all human. Just a little different.'

Mam and Dad. It's no coincidence that my parents have disappeared. They did something to them. Holly and Billy. They did something to them.

'Do you know where my parents are?' But my voice has become so weak that no-one hears me.

'Was that an egg?' says Tina.

'You got it, T,' says Billy, his two hands like guns. 'They're genetically engineered anti-personnel arthropods. We call 'em war bugs. You would not believe how difficult it was to get them here.'

Holly. She drove straight to my house. After Dad's office. She knew exactly where to go. I never told her.

Tina is talking. 'What do they do?'

Billy shrugs. 'Clearance.'

'Clearance?'

'Well, let's face it, Tina,' he says, 'you guys haven't exactly done a good job, have you?'

'What are you talking about? What do you mean?'

'What does he mean?' Holly turns and comes back down the camper to us. 'What does he mean?' Her voice is so full of venom. 'In the last fifty years, you've wiped out sixty per cent of all mammals, birds, fish and reptiles. Sea levels are rising. In twenty years, this –' She opens her arms. 'All of this will be under water. And you want to know if we've been surfing? Wake up, Tina!' She clicks her fingers in Tina's face.

It was an act, it was all an act. All those hours we spent surfing, all those stories Holly told about what they'd been doing over the winter. All that warmth, all those smiles. All fake, all fake.

'Where are my parents?' I still can't get my voice loud enough.

'War bugs,' says Tina. 'What do they do?

'Should have the planet cleared in less than a week,' says Billy.

'Cleared?' says Tina. 'What does that mean?'

'I think you know what it means, T,' says Billy. 'No more emissions, no more pollution, no more plastic.'

'No more people,' says Tina.

Billy does his two-handed gun thing again. 'Bingo!'

'He killed them. He killed them already.'

'What? Who?' says Billy, who's finally heard me.

'My parents. You've killed them, haven't you?'

Billy is shaking his head. 'No, dude, couldn't do that. We're pretty sure their vital signs are being monitored. If we snorked them, that'd give the game away. Cavalry would be here in hours.'

'Where are they?'

'They're with the rest of the eggs,' he says. 'They'll go the same time as everyone else.'

'Go?' Tina and I say this at the same time.

'Look, guys,' says Billy, half apologetically. 'We left the planet in your hands. You were in charge and you made a mess of it. It's dying, it's gonna die unless someone does something. And that someone is us. Right, babes?'

'Stop, stop stop!' Tina holds her hands up. 'What are you talking about? What do you mean "We left the planet in your hands?"'

'Oh, right, yeah,' says Billy, standing up and scratching his stubble. 'Babes, you're better at history than me. You wanna take this one?'

Holly's been standing there, leaning against the counter, her arms folded, looking at us with that same awful coldness.

'The first and only real alien abduction,' says Holly, 'happened 247,000 years ago. Five hundred humans were taken from Earth. At the time, there were many different sentient species in our sector – Kolates, Murdi, Vanchilians and so on. But humans are exceptionally adaptable, and we did very well. There are trillions of us out there now in various sectors. Earth is our ancestral home. You ...' she drops her head and stares hard at me and Tina, 'meaning those who were left here on Earth, have been doing nothing but trying to destroy it for the last two hundred years. That's why I'm here.'

This can't be happening. It can't. It just can't. I feel like my brain is in a cement mixer. 'So, like, you've put these eggs into the mines, and –'

'You should see these guys work!' Billy whistles and shakes his head. 'They lock onto human DNA. You can't hide from them. They can get through a magnorum plate ten metres thick in, like, seven seconds or something. Then it's –' He claps his hands together and makes a squelching noise. 'There was this famous incident on a planet called Pancho. Eight hundred of these bugs wiped out forty billion people in, like, six weeks. And the good news is you guys just don't have the tech to deal with them.'

Bugs. Mutant killer insects.

'What did you do with my parents?'

'Yeah, I'm sorry about that, dude. See, Martin, they're sentinels. Well, that's their official title, but really, they're more like mall cops. No offence, man, but they're the worst. It's their job to keep us out. But we got them before they tagged us, right, babes?' He holds up a hand for a high five but Holly ignores him.

She turns to me. 'You need to go.'

'So they do have a job here. They were protecting us. From you.'

Billy shrugs. 'Pretty much.'

'Why did you bring Martin up from the mine, then?' says Tina. 'Why did you help us if all you wanted to do was kill us?'

'Oh, we couldn't blow our cover, T,' he says, frowning. 'Had to fit in, play the part, yeah?'

'You need to leave now,' Holly says again.

My mind is still spinning. Part of it is trying to process all of this, but it keeps getting drowned out by one thought. Mam and Dad. They're not the bad guys. They're not the bad guys. And they're not dead. Not yet. I turn to Tina. Her face is blotchy. She's panting like a dog. We lock eyes and then she glances at the shelf just inside the door, and I get it. I get it. The blue-light thing. The thing Holly used to kill the egg. We need it. We need it.

I move from the bed towards the door, so it looks as if I'm going to leave. Holly, who's been standing at the shelf, has to move sideways to where I've just been standing. Now both of them are by the bed, to the left of the door.

Suddenly Tina flies at Billy and starts thumping him wherever she can land a blow. On his head, his shoulders, his face, his back. He lets her punch and slap and kick him without trying to defend himself. Holly sighs and shakes her head but doesn't do anything about it.

I'm there now, I'm right there at the shelf. I can see the thing, the blue-light thing, out of the corner of my eye. But if I try to take it at the wrong moment, Holly will see me.

'Hey,' says Billy, 'it's OK little one, it's OK. I know, I know.'

The tenderness makes Tina crazy. 'Shut up!' she screams at him. 'Shut your ugly face!'

'Tina, Tina, come on.' I move closer to them, I look like I'm trying to pull her away. And that's it, that's the opportunity. Without looking down, I lower my hand onto the blue-light thing. It's chunky and has straps, like a watch or a fitness tracker. I slip it from the shelf and into my pocket.

Tina gives up and stands there panting.

'When is all of this going to happen?' They don't hear me the first time so I say it again.

Billy shrugs. 'You've got six or seven hours.'

'Seven hours? Till they hatch?'

'Get out,' says Holly. 'Now.'

I can't help staring at her. I feel like she's the first person I've ever seen clearly. I realise that all the other summers they've been here, I wasn't really paying them any attention. I was only looking at *me* with them. All I cared about was how cool I was managing to be and desperately trying to come up with something clever to say. And all the time, I missed that hard gleam in her eyes. Each time she turned away, each time she watched us walk back up the beach to get the bikes, that smile would collapse into this awful sneer. She hates us. She's always hated us.

Tina turns and runs from the van. I don't catch up with her until we're nearly back at the car park. Though it's still early, there are plenty of people about. I can feel them looking over.

'Tina! T! Wait!'

When she turns, I think she's going to hit me. 'It's my fault. I ruined everything.' She's shaking. 'I broke the signal thing and I ruined it. I've ruined everything.'

'Tina, Tina, stop.'

'If I had let you send the signal, we'd be fine, we'd all be fine. Now it's over, everything is over.'

8. FOOTBALLS

Turns out Tina had known where I was, not because of some amazing telepathy but because, ages back, we set our phone locator apps to find each other's phones in case one of them got lost or something. Sitting in her room, she was able to follow my progress from my house to Maher's field. The signal disappeared as I went down into the mine, but by then she knew enough to get Cool Billy – well, Evil Billy now, I suppose – on the case.

Tina doesn't want to take Enda down the mine with us. 'Even supposing he can climb down OK, he might just wander off and get lost.'

I'm shaking my head. 'No, T, no way. He's in there, he knows what's going on. Two snakes. It wasn't a coincidence. And three times he's looked at me, right at me. You saw that.'

'Yeah, but …'

'Why are you resisting this? Why don't you see this?'

Suddenly, we're on the edge of another fight, and I just can't deal with that. Mutant killer insects from outer space? Fine, just no more fighting with Tina.

'Look,' she says, 'let's just give him the choice. Let's just bring him back to his house and see what he does.'

'Fine.'

Enda lives up on the coast road, just across from the cliffs and the Brenner Stack. But when we bring him up there, he won't go in. When Tina and I pedal into the drive, he just sits on the saddle at the gate and stares at the ground.

'Come on, Enda, time to go home,' she says, but he ignores her. She goes back out and tugs at his shoulder, but he shrugs her off. Next thing his little sisters appear from the side of the house. I can never remember which is Saoirse and which is Ciara. They usually ignore me anyway.

'Tina, can I do your hair?'

'Not now, Ciara. *Enda!*'

He's taken off, down the hill towards my house.

'Enda! Come on!'

But he's gone.

We turn to leave.

The smaller one – Saoirse, I think – is staring at me. She's so like Enda it's uncanny. 'You're like Batman and Robin,' she says. 'Only Tina's Batman.'

'Pleeeease?' says Ciara.

'Later,' says Tina, 'when we drop Enda home. Tell your mammy we'll be back later.'

'So long, Robin,' says Saoirse.

When we get to my house, we find him in the train shed, staring vacantly at the little engine going through the model village, over the bridge, through the tunnel, along the back wall and back again. Around and around and around.

'We're going to be gone a while, Enda, OK?' says Tina.

He doesn't respond.

'Enda,' I say, 'if we don't get back, just go home, OK?'

No response. I look at Tina, who shrugs and turns to leave.

***

We edge past the huge rock that extends out into the tunnel, the place where I found the egg, then we come to the first side tunnel, which leads down and to the left. I'm in front, holding Tina's phone in my gloved hand. Before we left, we downloaded a map of the tunnels from the Glencooper mining heritage site.

'Pretty sure this one is a dead end,' I say.

Soon the going gets muddier, and the puddles get bigger and longer. We pass the place where I dropped my phone, and not long after that, we hit a puddle that just doesn't end. Shining the torches on the black water, we can see that the entire way ahead of us is flooded. How deep? Who knows?

'Eee-uck,' says Tina, as the water flows in over the tops of her wellies. And I feel it then as the water climbs to our knees. This slows us down because we can't see the floor, and who knows what might be lurking under the surface? Stones or fallen timbers or holes or anything. The water gets a lot deeper really quickly. It's like wading into an underground river. When it gets to our waists, Tina has to take off her rucksack and carry it in front of her like a baby to keep it from getting wet. The cold pushes up into my spine. It's a hopeless sort of cold that makes you feel like you'll never be warm again, like there's no such thing as the sun. I can hear Tina's uneven breathing over the *swoosh swoosh* of our bodies pushing through the water, and the constant, irregular *drip drip drip* from the ceiling.

I can't help but remember some of the stories we learned in school about the mines. There was a big accident in eighteen seventy something, where thirteen people were buried alive after a shaft collapsed. There was one survivor, a guy who was trapped in the foetal position for nearly forty hours before rescuers got to him.

I try not to think about what we're trying to do here, what we're trying to prevent, because it jams up my brain, like a stick shoved into a spinning bicycle wheel. I try not to think about what happened down here yesterday. Was it even a stroke? What if it happens again? What if I collapse into the water and drown because Tina can't pull me out?

'Shut up, brain,' I say out loud.

'What?'

'Nothing.'

Holly's blue-light death-ray thing is strapped to my wrist. I keep glancing down at it, trying to remember which button she pressed, which one shoots out that killing blue light.

Behind me, Tina stumbles but doesn't fall.

'You OK?' I ask.

'Arms tired.'

'Here, you take the phone. I'll take the bag.'

We swap over and Tina goes in front. Now the tunnel turns and there's an opening to our left. She shines the light into it. It's just the same. Water and rock.

'This one seems to join up with another coming down from Garrenturk,' she says.

I'm scanning the ancient frame at the mouth of the tunnel when my eye falls on something etched into the timber. At first I think it's graffiti, but it isn't. 'Look!'

It's a stickman inside a circle – kind of like that Leonardo da Vinci drawing – except a heavy dark line runs through the circle, cutting the stickman in two. I've seen it before but I can't think where.

'Holly,' says Tina. 'She's got a necklace with that on it.'

Without another word, she pushes into the new tunnel. It runs straight for a few hundred metres before another opening appears on the left. The same symbol is printed on the timber here, so we take it. Almost immediately there's another turn with the same symbol.

I see Tina stumble again, but again she doesn't fall. 'Watch out!' she calls. 'Gets deeper.'

She's only a few metres ahead of me, but I can only see her head and shoulders now. She's walking with her hands on top of her head, like a prisoner of war. There's no way I can get through without the bag getting wet.

'Tina, I –'

She calls back, 'No, it's OK, it gets shallower.'

So I hold the bag up, grunting with the strain of it, feeling it scrape against the ceiling of the tunnel. Then I hear Tina splashing forward.

'This is it!' she calls.

I see it, just ahead. The water ends and the tunnel feeds into a big open space. Circular. Massive. Filled with eggs. Hundreds of them, glowing green, piled like footballs.

'Mam! Dad!' I drop the bag and pause for half a second, hoping for a response. When it doesn't come, I take off, running around the huge pile of eggs. The place is a cavern. High and wide and round. But warm, warm like a stuffy room.

'Mam! MAM!' The sound echoes around the chamber, which must be, I don't know, twenty metres across. I'm trying to look in all directions at once. 'Can you see them? I can't see them!'

I've circled the whole thing now. I'm back to where Tina is standing and there's no sign of them.

'He said they were here, Tina. Where are they?' And I'm off again. I've pulled off the head torch and am holding it in my hand, scanning and scanning the rows of eggs.

Tina calls. 'Martin, here!'

I race back and she's scooping eggs out of her way. For a minute I can't see why; then I see skin, fingers, a human hand – there among the eggs just a little way in from the edge of the pile. I throw myself in beside her and start tossing eggs out of the way. They roll and slide across each other with hollow metallic sounds.

My father's arm, his shoulder. I can't tell if the warmth is him or just heat from the eggs. I pull off my gloves and squeeze his shoulders. 'Dad! Dad! Wake up!'

He doesn't respond.

His face is eerily green in the light. Eyes closed, mouth closed. I press two fingers to the side of his neck, like they showed us in Scouts, but my hands are shaking so much, I can't tell. 'Tina, is there a pulse? Can you feel a pulse?'

I stand back to let her in and she picks up his wrist, holds it between finger and thumb and presses the fingers of her other hand against his throat. I go still watching her. Her eyes lock on mine, and for the longest time she doesn't move, doesn't speak.

'Tina!'

'Shhhh.' She looks away.

Stop, don't look away.

Then she speaks. 'It's there, I can feel it, I can feel it. It's faint but I can feel it.'

'Are you sure?'

'Yes, definitely.'

We start tossing more eggs aside. Mam's got to be here too, got to be. The eggs are clinking and sliding all over the place and we're slipping around on top of them.

Again, it's Tina that finds her, and by the time I get over, she's got her two fingers pressed to my mother's throat. She looks like she's sleeping, lips slightly parted, hair a mess.

'Stop moving,' says Tina. 'I can't concentrate.'

So for a second time, I hang there, thinking, *I can't be lucky a second time, I can't be, I don't deserve it.*

'It's there, Martin, it's there, she's alive. They're both alive. They must have drugged them or something.'

And now we're throwing eggs every which way. Mam has on her coat as if she's just walked out of the house, and like Dad, she's warm to the touch.

With Tina at his shoulders, I grab Dad's legs and haul him slowly over the eggs. I'm hoping that all this manhandling will wake him but there's no response. His breathing is so shallow, I can't even see his chest rise and fall. Mam makes a small sound as we pull her clear.

'Mam! It's Martin! Can you hear me?' I take her hand and squeeze it, but she doesn't squeeze back. She makes no other sound.

Once we get them out, I take Holly's device from my wrist. It's chunky, with a perfectly square screen, which is black with purple lines down the sides. It's got six buttons: four down one side, two down the other. I hold it at arm's length, aiming at a group of eggs that have rolled against the wall, trying each of the buttons in turn. Nothing happens.

'Try combinations,' says Tina.

So I do, and there's a beep followed by voices. We're suddenly raked by light from the device. I cry out and nearly drop the thing. Billy is there in front of us. I mean, right there on the dusty floor, grinning, in shorts and a T-shirt. He's not looking at us – he's looking past us at something. I whirl around but there's no-one there.

'Babes! You filming this?' He's grinning and a little sheepish.

We hear Holly's voice from somewhere. 'I need to do a test run.'

'It's a hologram,' says Tina, 'a hologram. They're not really here.'

She's right, I realise, but it's hard to dispute the evidence of my senses. It looks as if he's right here in the chamber, laughing and making stupid faces. The screen on the device is awake now, and there are symbols and pictures glowing dimly on it.

'Can I see?'

I pass it to Tina. 'Careful.'

She taps the screen and Billy disappears. Now Holly appears in his place, dressed head to toe in what looks like a wetsuit. She's got the coolest helmet I've ever seen under her arm.

'Just … that's perfect, Billy, hold it there.' She turns to the camera. 'My name is Holliam Mathise Arundel. I am a volunteer with the Earth Restoration Project. I am speaking to you from a subterranean facility in Earth's northern hemisphere.'

This is the scary version of Holly. She holds herself tall and straight like a soldier. Her voice is deep, her face *so* serious. And again, that hardness, that steel in her eyes.

'For many years, we in the ERP have argued that the destruction of the Earth's biosphere at the hands of its human occupants required urgent and decisive action.

The politicians have argued and debated and made resolutions but they have failed to take action. Now, with Earth's environment at the point of collapse, we in the ERP are taking the decision out of the politicians' hands. *We* are taking decisive action.'

Holly pauses for a moment.

'I am about to lay down the final set of war-bug eggs. In two weeks, Earth will be restored. No more arguments, no more waiting for those in power to do something about it. These lazy, stupid, malignant caretakers will be no more. We have had the courage and vision to do what no-one else would do. Over and out.'

She puts on the helmet, which is black shot through with purple zigzags. Then she dissolves into a single point of light, which then disappears.

'Oh God.' Tina's blinking, staring at the place where Holly was just standing.

I take the device from her hands and scroll through the pictures and symbols, looking for that killing blue light, but the thing just runs onto a new hologram.

A guy in a dark suit materialises on the floor of the cavern. He's got big sideburns and long hair. He's talking, as if to a camera. 'Now we return again to that theft of contraband biotech from the storage facility at the Bromi Calzar installation. In an unprecedented move, General Io has broadcast a public appeal for help in its recovery. The stolen biotech, which had been slated for demolition –'

'It's a news report,' says Tina.

Now the news guy is gone and a woman in a military uniform appears. 'We are particularly concerned that the arthropod eggs may be smuggled off-world and deployed in a culture which lacks the facility to deal with the threat. These war bugs, as they're called, are among biotech outlawed by both the Mindor Confederation and the Anterior Planets under the terms of the Ythaca-Nascics Agreement. This tech was specifically designed to target human subjects and was used extensively in the infamous Pancho genocide, when an estimated 800 of these arthropods destroyed the entire human population of 40.2 billion.'

The long-haired guy comes back and says, 'Viewers may find this footage distressing.'

It's like a tiny city has magically appeared in the chamber. We both step back to get out of the way. The buildings are tall and beautiful; there's curving blue steel and glass everywhere. But some of the buildings are blackened and crumbling and smoke billows from them. Cars, packed end to end, inch along the street, and the footpaths are crowded with people. There are thousands – maybe tens of thousands – all moving slowly in one direction. Then there are screams, and suddenly something is there with the people, something we can't see because their images are pixellated. People are running, scattering in all directions. Some of them take to the air. I see them zipping upwards, but small, hazy clusters of pixels dart towards them and there's a horrible wet noise. Clumps of distorted images – of what must be blood and body parts – drop to the street. Half the hologram is clouded now as hundreds of these things descend on their human victims, and though we can't see what happens, there is enough movement to leave us in no doubt. The screams are horrifying.

Tina's hands are clamped over her ears. 'Turn it off!'

My hands are shaking. I tap things at random. The volume rises suddenly and the hologram swells, so that we are now standing in the middle of this terrible slaughter; then, just as suddenly, it dies. The image disappears, leaving only the fading echo of a single scream, and when that fades, we're both standing there, panting.

Tina takes the device from me. 'She just, she just grabbed it out of the cupboard and fired it. She didn't have time to scroll through screens or anything, so it must be these buttons.'

She turns the base of the device towards the wall and begins testing combinations of buttons. What happens next happens quickly. There is no burst of blue light. Instead, Tina cries out and drops the device.

'What? What is it?'

'A sh– a shock. An electric shock.' She's flexing her fingers and rubbing her arm.

Suddenly Billy is there in front of us. Tina and I move towards each other instinctively.

'Hey, guys! Sorry to zap you, T! Automated security response. Couldn't allow you to access the snork ray, obviously,' Billy goes on. 'So that's disabled. Kudos to you.' He brings his hands together and bows. 'Stealing my K-band like that. Took us *waaaay* too long to figure out what happened to it. I've put it in self-destruct mode remotely. Anyway, we're going off-planet until the clean-up operation is over. Man, I really can't wait to see this place again! Gonna miss you guys.' He salutes, then the image swirls and shrinks into a single point of white light at the base of the wristband on the floor. The light goes out, and as I stare at it, the device liquefies. Liquefies. One minute it's small and solid, the next it's a dark blob on the floor with a wisp of smoke rising from it. For a moment, we're frozen, unable to drag our eyes from it. Then I fall to my knees and reach out to it. It's a warm, shapeless blob, like molten wax or something.

'It's dead,' I whisper. 'Dead.'

I look up at Tina, who's shaking her head slowly. The death ray was all we had. It's gone. She rushes to her rucksack and starts dragging things out – food and blankets and tools.

'Here!' she says, lobbing a hammer towards me. 'Just let's at least try to smash them. Now, while they're eggs.'

She's got a hatchet. She grabs the nearest egg, steadies it with one hand and, with the other, brings the hatchet down hard. There's a sound like a gong being struck and a spark flies upwards. The egg skitters across the floor, collides with two others, then spins off like a pinball. I rush over, scoop it up and turn it over and over. There's not so much as a scratch. But still I pick up the hammer and go to work on the nearest one. The clangs ring out but the hammer doesn't even mark it.

'It's not working, Tina.'

She's hacking into eggs and they're ricocheting about the floor like huge marbles.

'Tina!'

And now she just flings away the hatchet and roars at the top of her voice, and then roars again and again. At the end of it, she drops down on her knees among the scattered eggs, exhausted and panting.

9. LOBSTER

Larry is this huge inflatable lobster that the three of us clubbed together to buy a couple of years ago. Messing around with Larry at the beach is the most fun thing ever. Or at least it was the most fun thing ever. Then my parents found out about it and freaked out.

I drag him out of the rucksack now and start pumping him up. When I get tired, Tina takes over.

The plan is to use Larry as a stretcher and float my parents out on his back. Getting them on is a nightmare. Tina stands in the water of the tunnel, trying and failing to get a grip on the smooth, slippery plastic. The other end is up on the dry floor of the chamber. I grab Mam under her arms and drag her backwards, but the lobster-stretcher just keeps sliding sideways and threatening to dump both of us into the water. Eventually, after I don't know how many goes, we settle her in place, but because we have to lay her over on one side to make room for Dad, the whole thing wants to capsize. So Tina can't help me with Dad at all. She has to stand in the water, frozen half to death, and hold the lobster steady while I drag him onto it inch by inch.

When we get going, progress is slow. I go in the front, Tina at the back. The mineshaft is too narrow in places and we have to pull and drag to get Larry through. And it's so cold. It feels like all my joints are slowly turning to ice. All I can hear is my own breathing and the lapping of the water and the scraping of the lobster against the rock.

I don't know how long we've been at it when Tina whispers, 'Wait, st–stop.'

'W–what?'

'Just, just stop.'

So we stop and go still. I can't hear anything for a minute, nothing but the dripping water, my chattering teeth and our uneven breathing. Then I hear it. A splash, a series of splashes. Splashes – not the irregular *drip drip drip* that's been running quietly in the background the whole time. 'What is that?'

Tina doesn't answer. I turn around and my torch lights the back of her head and a section of the dark water rippling behind us. I hear more splashes now, then a different sound, of moving water, and I realise that something about the movement in the water behind us is wrong. We've been still and unmoving for maybe half a minute. The ripples should have petered out, but they haven't. Tina crouches, then pulls off her head torch and holds it high over the water.

She cries out and next thing she's driving Larry into me so suddenly that I nearly stumble back into the water. 'Run!'

'What? What is it?'

'Just run, Martin!'

I know what it is, I know what it is.

The water is still waist-high, so it's like trying to run in a dream. My legs pump but I'm just not making enough progress. Tina is faster than me; she's pushing Larry into my back so that I can hardly stay on my feet, but I can't tell her to slow down. We're coming up on a turn, a T-junction. 'Is it right here?'

'Just run, Martin!'

I risk a glance behind. I'm trying to see into the water behind Tina, but my torch sweeps the ceiling and I see them. Three of them. Five or six feet long. Segmented like giant millipedes. Gleaming black. They scuttle upside down along the rock.

Tina scream-roars as we round the corner. I see her grab the hatchet from where we left it lying between my parents. Then it flashes in the torchlight and slams into the head of one of the giant maggots that swept down from the ceiling. There's a sound like eggs breaking and the thing splashes into the water. I try to drag Larry backwards, while Tina turns and swings two-handed at another one reaching for her from the ceiling. I get a brief glimpse of its black jaws snapping before the back of the hatchet collides with its head and the thing is slammed up into the ceiling.

The next turn comes seconds later. I go left instinctively. Tina's still swinging madly and screaming abuse at them. I can see they're coming at her from the walls, from the ceiling and along the top of the water. The light catches a shiny black shell skimming across the surface like a snake.

Tina is now maybe two metres behind the raft, and up ahead I see the water lapping up onto the mud. The end of the water. Who knew I'd be sorry to see it? Because how are we going to move Mam and Dad through the mud?

I grip the edge of the lobster as well as I can and heave, so that most of it is now out of the water. Then I stumble back down to Tina, grabbing the hammer as I go. I can see she's doing damage. There are bits of maggots floating on top of the water.

And now I see that she's not swinging two-handed any more. She's holding her right arm across her body. She's injured. I get up level with her. Blood. Her arm is soaked in blood.

'One of them got you.'

'Swap,' she says, pushing me to the other side of her. 'You take right, I'll take left.'

There are so many now, scuttling along the walls and ceiling, slithering across the top of the water. I bring the hammer down on one of these, but it's like hitting a balloon. The thing just slides away and dives underneath the water.

'You gotta get them on the wall,' Tina shouts. 'On the water's no good.'

And then I feel a sudden pressure on my thigh, and before I can pull away there's a second impact, like a punch, and I know I've been bitten. I just want to turn and run, but instead I swing at one coming down at me from the wall. I miss, and the thing drops into the water and disappears. Now I feel another punch to my leg and try to move out of the way and swing at it with the hammer. Tina roars and I look up to see that the far end of the passage we've just come through is jammed with them. Literally jammed with them. A writhing mass of maggots crammed between water and ceiling. And then they burst towards us in a rush of horrible black bodies, long feelers and snapping jaws. Tina grabs me and we half run, half stumble backwards out of the water.

Now, without a word said between us, we stoop and start dragging the raft, but it's no use. The mud clings to the bottom. The base of the lobster is like a suction cup.

'I'm not leaving them,' I say.

'I know,' says Tina, and we lock eyes for a minute. Her face is smeared in mud and blood, her hair plastered to her head.

We're screwed, we're totally screwed. There's no way we can fight them all. No way. I turn back towards the squirming mass of maggots and see that one of the ancient oak frames stands between us and them. If that was gone, the tunnel would probably collapse.

Now something weird happens. I'm about to dart forward and start hitting the frame with the hammer, but it's like, it's like I get stuck, like I'm stuck in a little bubble of time. I imagine the frame cracking, splintering, coming apart. I imagine the earth and rock tumbling down to block the tunnel. Now, I'm … I'm lifted off my feet and pulled towards it. I feel my body become light. *Wait. Stop.*

I blink, and the weight returns to my body. Though it has lasted less than half a second, Tina has seen it. She gets it. She gets it.

She wallops me on the shoulder. 'Get that timber out of here. Move it! Break it!'

The maggots are almost upon us now.

'MOVE IT!' Tina roars and hits me again.

Now I feel a pain at the base of my skull, and I grit my teeth against it and stare hard at the grey timber. It has to go. It has to go.

'Move it! MOVE IT!'

She swings back-handed at the nearest maggot, only I don't hear the crunch or the splash, if there is one, and I don't see what happens next, because all there is in the entire world is that grey timber. The pain accelerates up from the back of my head until it feels as if my brain is vibrating. Next thing, I realise my feet have left the ground and I'm hanging at an angle in the air. Then I'm moving, slowly, towards the beam and the surging mass of insects.

'NO!' Tina's voice cuts through everything. '*You* stay! Move the *beam*. MOVE IT!'

Yes. The beam. Move the beam. And I feel myself dropping into the mud. The pain makes me want to cry out and run away but, but … there's a crack, an echoing crack, and the timber starts to bulge unnaturally.

They're on us now, the first wave of maggots, and Tina is there near me somewhere, swinging and cutting. Another crack, then a flurry of smaller ones, then a small chunk of rock drops from the roof to the water. Tina roars and I know that all I've got is seconds, and when I feel myself being pulled from my feet, I widen my stance and think *I'm not going to move*, and when I do that, I feel my boots sink a little deeper in the mud, like I've suddenly gained fifty kilos. And the beam bulges towards me. More rock falls into the water, then a much larger chunk gives way and crashes in. I can feel the whole tunnel tremble. (One little part of my brain stands up and goes, 'I'm sorry? Excuse me? Exactly what is going on here?') And without meaning to, without deciding to, I roar at the beam and it snaps like dry twigs and jerks towards me. One of the supporting timbers comes away from the wall and in one movement, in one sudden movement, the whole left side of the tunnel lurches sideways, like ice calving from an iceberg. There's a sound like a mountain groaning, the tunnel collapses right in front of us, and all the displaced water surges towards us. I only have time to wrap my arms over my head before I'm completely submerged. Something hits me in the side – a piece of timber, a maggot, I don't know – and I can't keep my feet in the surge of water and I'm driven backwards. The wave subsides and I'm in a heap beside Larry, gasping for air.

I just collapsed the mine with my mind.

I. Just. Collapsed. The. Mine. With. My. Mind.

I'm sitting there in the mud, stunned, my ears ringing, my head aching. I look around, blinking. My torch is gone. Tina's has fallen. In the dim light it throws out from where it's landed in the mud, I see that something's wrong. There's a shape that might be hers and the sheen of a maggot's black shell tight upon it. I scramble up and see that there are two, no, three of them attacking her. They're wrapped about her body and neck. Tight, like constrictors. She can't breathe; she can't move her arms. I run up and grab the one that's wrapped about her neck. It's oily to the touch and its thrashing, crab-like legs squirm horribly in my hands. I have to dig my fingers in under its body, into the skin of her neck, to get a grip on it and yank it away from her. She gasps, air surging into her lungs as I grab the one that's wrapped about her middle. I rip it away and she gropes for the hatchet in the mud beside her and starts hacking at the third one, the one wrapped about her legs. In half a minute, the mangled remains of the maggots are twitching in the mud.

'Yeah!' Tina roars, shaking her fist at them. 'Yeah! You mess with us? You mess with us? How'd you like that?' And she aims a kick at one of the motionless black bodies at our feet.

My ears are still ringing. I can hardly hear her. Behind us, my parents are still prone on Larry's back … but, but it's not over. Tina's stance changes suddenly. She raises the hatchet again and turns away from the cave-in, back towards the base of the pit.

'What is it?'

But now I hear it. No, feel it. Beneath my feet. Vibrations. Something is coming towards us. My heart sinks.

How did they get behind us? There must be more of them. Of course there are. The tunnels are probably full of them. This is it, this is it, we're properly finished now.

Tina's grabbed my shoulder and is saying something, but my ears are still out of action, and the torch, which she's replaced on her head, is blinding me.

Next thing I hear her roar, 'Here! We're here!' And off she goes, limping, past Larry, back up the tunnel. And now I see light, several beams of light bouncing along the walls in front of us, and it's boots I'm feeling through the ground, and now I hear shouts and clinking metal. People. Humans. A rescue party? A rescue party!

10. LIFE CYCLE

When we finally get up out of the pit, Maher's field is lit up like it's the middle of the day, even though it's the middle of the night. Five or six sets of floodlights shine down on us, and from somewhere off to one side – I can't see through the glare – there's a round of applause as we climb out. Not for us, oh no, but for the rescue team who 'saved' us. There are two fire engines, a big red Civil Defence van, three ambulances and four or five garda cars. And a TV van.

Oh God.

Barely ten feet away, there's a guy from the telly with plastic hair and a suit. He's holding a microphone and talking into a camera. All I hear is '… that these are two very lucky teenagers to have been plucked from the jaws of death by …'

Oh God.

There's a crowd of – what? Forty? Fifty people? All clustered behind a police cordon. A genuine police cordon. Yellow tape with 'Do Not Cross' printed on it in black. I pick out a couple of people from school in the crowd, and I think I hear them laughing. I glance over at T, who, like me, is surrounded by firemen, cops and paramedics, and all I see is this mess of hair plastered to her face. For a minute I forget all about the imminent destruction of the human race and think that I'm going to die of embarrassment before the mutant insects can get me.

Mam and Dad are already gone to the hospital. We refused to move until they had been winched out. The emergency medical guy who looked them over down in the mine said that they were still breathing and that their hearts were beating. Dad groaned as they winched him up, but neither of them woke up.

Someone saw us. That's what happened. Someone passing by on the road saw us pulling back the boards and climbing down into the mine. They called the cops.

It's so unreal, it feels like someone else's dream. I am telekinetic. I can do telekinesis. I moved that wooden beam – a wooden beam that had held that shaft up for a hundred and fifty years. I broke it in two, just by thinking about it. *Just by thinking about it.* It's thrilling and terrifying at the same time. And behind all this excitement and terror, there's the certainty that I can't escape any more. They did lie to me. There is no polycythaemia vera, no rare disease. They made it all up to stop me from developing these, these abilities. I know they might have had their reasons, but as lies go, it's a pretty big one.

We're nearly at the ambulances when Tina's mother appears, along with all of her brothers and sisters, or most of them anyway, and they just swallow her up. I mean, there's this huge group hug. Mrs O'Reilly sees me and drags me into it, and it's kind of awkward but nice at the same time. Then we're marched on towards the ambulances. There's a doctor with red hair and a white coat at the back of one. He starts asking me if I'm OK and all that, then another white coat appears and drags a curtain on a metal frame around me and the doctor.

The ear-ringing is gone, but it's like I can actually feel my brain. It feels like someone dug it out and ran it under the cold tap for a minute before snapping it back in place. *I collapsed the tunnel with my brain. I ripped out a timber frame by thinking about it.* I almost laugh, but it comes out like a sob, and now it's all I can do to stop actually crying.

'You OK?' the doctor says.

I nod. Can't trust my voice.

He flutters around me, shining lights in my eyes, listening to my heart and lungs and all that. He spots the wounds on my legs where the giant maggots bit me, and I have to struggle out of my soaking tracksuit bottoms so he can deal with them. There's a lot of blood, but the wounds are short and clean and don't look that deep.

'What happened here?' he asks.

I just shrug.

But it's wrong. Something is wrong. They were too easy to kill. We managed to fight off dozens of them with household tools. I know we couldn't actually see the horrible things in the hologram, but whatever was hiding behind those pixels, it wasn't the things we just fought. So did Holly screw up? Maybe the eggs aren't what she thought they were? And then, just as the doctor begins dabbing at the wounds with cotton wool, I get it.

This little phrase pops into my head, a phrase from biology class. The lifecycle of an insect. *Egg, larva, pupa, adult*. It repeats, like a nursery rhyme. *Egg, larva, pupa, adult*. Those things? They were larvae. They're not the end of the story. They're going to pupate. They're going to pupate like caterpillars, and when they're done, the adults will come out. And the adults will be those awful pixellated things in the hologram. *They're* what we have to fear.

'OK, Martin?'

'Sorry, what?'

'We're going to take you in for the night, just to keep you under observation. No need to worry. I don't think there's anything wrong, but you've been through quite an ordeal, and I'm sure you'd rather be close to your parents in any case.'

I look blankly at him. 'Yeah ... yeah, sure.'

He stands over me, indicating that I should climb into the back of the ambulance.

'Ah ... could we just wait a few minutes, just to get some air? It was pretty stuffy down there.'

'Of course.' He tosses his stethoscope in the back and goes.

It's not over. We have to go back there. They're vulnerable now, as larvae. We've got to get back down there. We've got to get back down there and ... burn them or something. Fire. If we could fill the chamber with fire, that could destroy them. But we've got to move fast.

Though I can't hear her voice, I realise that Tina is probably behind the curtain set up around the back of the ambulance parked right beside mine. I go down on all fours and, yeah, there are the yellow wellies and the doctor's feet and, I guess, T's mother's feet. I stand up and move closer to them, trying to filter out the noises from the rest of the field.

'Can you turn your head to one side, Christina, please?' It's the doctor. 'Just look at the light, thank you.'

Alongside this, though much more quietly, I hear Mrs O'Reilly. She's … making calming sounds, I think.

'It's OK, pet, you're all right now. You're all right there now, don't cry.'

It's only when I hear this that I realise the snuffling sounds that have been there all along are Tina crying. Tina never cries. Never.

I hover, listening to the sobbing and T's mother hushing and tutting and stuff. The doctor says the same thing he said to me, that he's going to bring her to hospital just to keep an eye on her. I lean in to make sure I don't miss what she says, but I hear nothing. Sobs and sniffs.

Of course this is how she's going to react. Of course it is. Those things nearly killed her. She couldn't breathe. She was nearly strangled to death by a giant alien maggot. If that's not going to mess with your head, what is? She's been through hell. And I want her to come back there with me?

Yes, that's exactly what I want. But I can't ask her. I just can't. I'll have to go alone. I have no choice. Alone. Is

111

that even possible? I need paraffin or petrol or something, and lots of it, plus a way to get back down there. And fast.

I pull back on my tracksuit bottoms and slip my feet into the boots, which feel yucky. I push the curtain to one side and check both ways. The entrance to the mine is on one side, with the cops, the firemen, the TV crew and the crowd. To the other side, the emptiness and darkness of the rest of the field. And now I feel so horribly lonely. I get this desperate urge to go back and curl up inside the ambulance. This should not be my job. It just shouldn't. It's not fair.

I can still hear Tina's sobs. Even though it's the last thing my feet want to do, I turn towards the darkness and slip quietly down along the side of the ambulance. I hover there for a minute, waiting for my eyes to adjust, and maybe also waiting for some brilliant idea to strike me, something so genius that the need to go disappears and everything will be all right, but it doesn't come, so I walk deeper into the darkness and pick my way up to the slope towards the little clump of trees where we left the bikes. I don't pause for a last look but feel my way in.

It's so dark here, and there are so many brambles and briars and branches, that it takes me far too long to find the way through, but when I do get there, the bikes are just where we left them.

I'm back home in maybe twenty minutes. I leave the bike in the trees and let myself in the back door. I don't turn on any lights, but move about the place like a mouse, listening for a car turning in to the drive.

Standing by the table in the darkened kitchen, I go still. I have to try again. I just have to. And I barely think it – I mean, it's the vaguest little half thought – but the table rises smoothly until it's hovering there just below the ceiling. And now I laugh, a real laugh, my heart hammering at the joy of it. I lower the table slowly, but it still clatters onto the floor, and I catch my breath, but there's no-one to hear. And then I try it. I swallow hard and in the darkness of the kitchen I rise up into the air, smoothly and effortlessly, until I can reach up and touch the ceiling. Then I slowly circle the table, half a metre off the ground. And for half a moment I forget about everything else and all I can feel is the thrill of it. I am flying. I can fly.

All those arguments we had over the years about superpowers. Tina wanted invisibility, Enda wanted the ability to teleport, but I wanted flight.

I feel a pain gather in the back of my head, just like I did in the mines. A dull pain that rises up slowly but surely, and I know it won't stay a dull pain for long. There's a price to pay. You don't just get to soar. There's a price.

I put on dry clothes and eat cheese, then root out a backpack and start collecting things I might need: rope, a penknife, matches – which I wrap up in a freezer bag in case I get wet again. I find another hammer and a bike light. The hammer and the torch I brought into the mine stayed down there. What else?

I'm in the garage looking for containers to put petrol in when I hear an engine, then the crunch of gravel.

Headlights sweep the garage door, sending light underneath it. I go still. The engine roars, and the car seems to jerk forward. Or is it even a car? It sounds bigger. There's a spray of gravel against the door, and then it goes quiet. A door opens, a big door. Definitely not a car. It doesn't close again. Feet hit the gravel. I'm waiting to hear the doorbell, but it doesn't ring, and I guess that they're coming around to the back. I pick my way as quietly as I can to the back door of the garage, which I'd left ajar, and quietly as I can, I ease it shut, all the time listening for footsteps, watching the window for the telltale flash of a torch. Next thing I know, the door is opening. The door I'm standing at. I step back against the wall and hold my breath. The door pivots inwards until it's wide open, but there's no flashlight.

'Martin?'

'Tina? What are you doing? Who did you –?'

Before I can finish, I get a punch into the stomach.

'You ghosted me, Martin. You ghosted.'

I straighten up slowly, holding the door for support.

'You don't ghost, Martin. You don't do that. We don't do that to each other.'

A bit of me wants to get mad. I'm already sore and exhausted and sick with nerves without having to deal with a punch in the gut. 'I just … I thought you'd been through enough.'

'Oh, did you?' She slips into full sarcasm mode. 'You thought poor little Tina was too weak to take the fight to the beasties? Is that what you thought?'

'Who drove you here, Tina? Who did you tell?'

'You thought you could take them on your own, I suppose. You thought –'

'Who did you tell, Tina? Who's out there?'

'No-one.'

'So who …?' I get a horrible intuition and push past her out the door, then dash forward to the front of the house. 'Oh God, Tina.'

There, sitting on the gravel in front of my house is an ambulance.

11. AMMONIUM NITRATE

'If your folks are really security guards or something, like Billy said, then shouldn't they have weapons?'

Tina can't seem to figure out the gears. As soon as we build up a little speed, the engine starts whining and moaning. Half the time, when she tries to move the gearstick, there's a terrible grinding noise and the whole ambulance bucks and heaves like it's trying to throw us out, like it knows it's stolen and wants to get rid of us.

'I don't know,' I say, gripping the sides of the seat. 'I've never seen anything like that. Can we just slow down a bit?'

'I mean, think about it. You're protecting a planet – protecting a planet from people and things with really advanced tech. And you don't get weapons? It doesn't make sense.'

She changes gear again, kicking off another of those grinding bounces. I'm thrown forward, and somehow I hit the button for the blue lights and the siren. It's deafening. Anyone within five miles will be able to hear it.

'Turn it off!' Tina screams.

'I'm trying!'

I don't know which button I hit, so I'm slapping switches randomly. Which is how I manage to turn off the headlights just as we come to a blind turn in the road.

'Turn them on!' Tina roars, not even slowing down, and after a few scary seconds, the lights blaze on again and she has to swivel the wheel to keep us from ending up in the ditch. A thick branch clips one of the wing mirrors and it snaps clean off.

'Oh God.'

'Shut up, Martin.'

She's changed out of her wet clothes and into a set of surgical scrubs she found in a drawer in the back of the ambulance. They're about four sizes too big, and she still has the yellow wellies.

She thought that Holly had screwed up, that she had brought in the wrong eggs, but when I gave her my larvae theory she realised that that had to be it. They're babies, and what's coming next isn't going to be so easy to deal with. So we've got to move fast. We've got to get them while they're vulnerable. I wanted to use fire, I wanted to fill containers with petrol and somehow get it down there and set the place alight, but Tina, Tina's got another idea. It's a good idea, yes, but …

One of her brothers – Declan – works for Kerrigan's. They have a quarry a few kilometres from the village. They use rock breakers – enormous yellow machines with huge pneumatic chisels – to get the stone out of the ground. But if that doesn't work, Declan blasts it out. He drills deep holes in the rock face, puts explosives into the holes, clears the quarry and blows the rock to pieces. Three times, he's brought Tina along to show her these explosions, so she fancies herself a complete expert on blowing stuff up.

'The place will be empty,' she says. 'We break in, get the explosives, take them back to the mine. *Boom*. Planet saved.'

I don't bother replying. What's the point? I mean, the possibility of us actually stopping this and saving everyone is so remote that adding another impossible task to the list hardly matters. So, yeah, fine. Let's go steal dynamite.

The road straightens out and she glances sideways at me and goes, 'Oh my God, dude.'

'I know.'

'Oh my God.'

'I know, I know.'

'You broke that thing by just thinking about it.'

'Guess what else? I flew round the kitchen.'

'WHAT?' The ambulance swerves and I grab the sides of the seat again. 'You flew?'

'Yeah, Just a little bit.'

'Oh my God, dude!'

'I know.'

'Oh my God!'

I feel a little surge of relief, and I realise that part of me was afraid she might be jealous. In the light from the dashboard I can see the lines on her neck where the maggots tried to strangle her. I can feel the deadness in my thigh where they bit me. She did a lot more battling than me, so she must have more wounds. 'You OK?'

She half glances at me and nods.

'Your neck.'

Her hand goes to it. 'What, does it look weird?'

'No, but ... that was pretty hairy.'

She shakes her head. 'Don't think about it, just don't think about it. Not yet.'

The quarry is screened from the road by a high bank. The entrance itself kind of sneaks up on us. One second we're speeding down the road; the next, Tina hauls the wheel around and the ambulance skids sideways into the wide dusty area before the gate. The place is in darkness.

Before we left my house, I had thrown Dad's tools in the back of the ambulance. I find the bolt cutters quickly now and bring them to the quarry gate, which is held closed with a padlock and a big winding chain. I hover there with the chain in the jaws of the cutters. The night is vast and dark and silent.

'You sure about this?' I call back.

Tina's leaning out the driver's window. 'Hurry up!'

Going down that mine probably wasn't a crime. And ghosting the doctor, that probably wasn't a crime either. OK, yeah, stealing the ambulance was a crime, sure, but that was Tina's thing. Now, for the first time, I'm going to have to cross a line. And I realise that if all of this works, if we actually do succeed in preventing the destruction of the human race, we're still screwed. What does success look like? It means ending up in a juvenile detention centre with arsonists and muggers and trainee gangsters who'll probably eat me alive.

119

Snap. I close the bolt cutters and the chain unwinds and clatters to the ground.

Tina drives the ambulance in and I close the gates after her. Then she leads the way to the line of prefabs just inside the fence. She's still got her torch. I've got the bike light from home.

'It's this one,' she says, testing the door, which is of course locked. But it's a flimsy prefab door. I drag over Dad's lump hammer. Before I can do too much thinking about it, I swing the hammer at the area just below the handle, where the lock meets the frame, and the door bursts open first time. But as it does, we're suddenly bathed in purple light. Alarm, there's an alarm. Right above our heads, just over the door. How could we have missed it? It's silent but it flashes angrily across the concrete and prefabs and the big yellow lorries parked across from us.

'What are we going to do now?' I whisper fiercely, but she's already darted inside and turned on the lights.

She calls over her shoulder. 'We go in, we get what we need, and we get out.'

There are white bags stacked to head height and shelves to one side filled with an assortment of things: wire, small red boxes labelled 'Blasting Caps' and what look like stubby red candles. Tina is sweeping these into a shopping bag.

'We'll need about ten of those sacks,' she says, 'maybe twelve.'

She drags the bag she's filled outside, and I pull the first of the white sacks from the top of the pile.

'Careful!' she calls. 'That's ammonium nitrate.'

This means nothing to me, but I heave the bag carefully into my arms and follow her to the ambulance, where I ease it onto the floor next to Tina's shopping bag. Back and forth we go until we've got about eight bags loaded.

I'm back at the prefab, about to lift another one, when I hear it. A high-pitched whirring noise, like an insect.

'Tina?' I whisper, but she's still back at the ambulance and doesn't hear.

The whirr gets rapidly louder and now, suddenly, there it is, hovering in the air over the concrete. My legs go weak. For a moment I think it's one of those things that we couldn't see in the news report, one of those mutant killer insects, and that I'm about to die horribly, but it's not. It's some sort of spaceship. Long and sleek and shaped like an electric razor, but no bigger than a helicopter. A metallic blue light circles rapidly about its undercarriage.

Maybe, I think, maybe the signal did get out. Maybe this is the cavalry arriving to save the day.

'Tina!' There's no sign of her.

The alarm's purple light continues to spin crazily about the concrete, and now, with the blue lights of the descending spaceship, the place is lit up like a nightclub.

It's weird. You'd expect a roar of engines, you'd expect a wind from the grey fins at the back of the thing, but there's nothing like that. Apart from that insect-like whine, there's no sound at all, and it seems to drop through the night without disturbing the air around it. Then, just when it's about to touch down, a dull yellow light flares along its length. I have the impression that it's somehow gotten *smaller*. The darkness suddenly gets thicker, and for a moment the ship seems to, well, disappear. I blink, and when I open my eyes, it's gone, and sitting on the concrete in its place is a bright orange VW van.

Holly and Billy.

The door slides back and Billy steps out. He's dressed in a black uniform just like the one Holly wore in the hologram.

'Martin! Explosives! Wow! That's such a great idea. Always said you were the smartest guy in town. Where's T?' He looks around.

'What do you want?' It's a stupid question, I know, but I can't think of anything else.

'See, dude, we realised we couldn't leave anything to chance. Like I say, if there was a way, I mean, you'd find it. I know you would.'

'How did you find us?'

Billy turns back. 'My K-band? That you guys stole? Leaves a little security marker on your fingers.' He holds up what looks like a phone. 'Tracked you with this.'

'Out of the way, Billy.' Holly appears. She's holding something in front of her, pointing something at me, *aiming* something at me.

I do what everybody does when that happens. I hold up my hands. 'Wait, wait, please –'

Next thing, Tina appears from nowhere and barrels into Holly, who slams against Billy, and they all go flying. I turn to run, and there's a sound like giant scissors snapping closed.

Now the world lights up, and a split second later there's an almighty bang and a rush of air. I find myself on the ground, my arms around my head, scootching backwards along the concrete. Something slams into the ground alongside me. I open my eyes and there's Dad's lump hammer, half buried in the concrete. I can read the label, 'Property of David Ryan', on the handle.

The prefabs have erupted into flame. There's smoke everywhere. I half crawl, half run to the row of lorries parked opposite while bits of charred timber and plastic rain down around me. Once I get clear of the yard, I turn back to see the van gone and the spaceship rising slowly into the air. Billy and Holly clearing out before the rest of the world arrives to see what's going on.

'Tina!'

Thick black smoke billows from the prefabs. I can feel the heat from here, maybe twenty metres away. Dancing tongues of fire throw light up the trees behind the burning buildings. The air is foul. I breathe into the crook of my arm and squint into the smoke, trying to see where she's gone. Holly must have hit the ammonium nitrate – she must have fired into it with her gun. The gun she nearly killed me with. I bat that thought away before it can take hold.

Tina. They didn't shoot her, did they? She was no closer to the explosion than I was, but … I see the hammer again, where it landed, and the spiderweb of cracks in the concrete about it. What if she got hit by flying debris? What if she was blown clear but is lying somewhere, breathing in smoke? What if Holly managed to shoot her before they took off?

The blue lights of the spaceship disappear overhead and I dart out, keeping low, calling her name, then burying my face in the crook of my arm again. About six metres from the prefabs, the heat drives me back. The smoke stings my eyes but there's no sign of Tina. Wisps of burning plastic drift down through the smoke.

I'm circling back towards the ambulance when I catch movement by the gate. Lights – hazy through the smoke. Headlights, I realise. A car. Clinking sounds. Someone is untangling the chain that I left piled about the bottom of the gate to give the impression it was locked. A thought strikes me. It's Mam and Dad. They've woken up and they've found us and they're going to make everything right. It's a crazy thought; it can't be them, it just can't. But what if it is?

The smoke is the only thing hiding me, so I dart towards the quarry machinery, which stands opposite the gate and towers above everything else. It's got huge metal struts, conveyor belts and a great yawning funnel. The firelight dances eerily on its flaking yellow and blue paint. I run beneath it and crouch in the darkness behind a rusted metal frame.

The car arcs slowly into the yard, giving the fire a wide berth. I duck down as the headlights flare against the frame. Then, as it turns side on, I look out and see that it's a cop car.

Crap.

They were alerted by the alarm, I guess. The car goes as far as the yellow lorries, then arcs back, passes just in front of where I'm hiding and parks up right beside the ambulance, downwind of the fire.

Maybe Holly and Billy got Tina. They were armed and she wasn't. So what happened? They picked themselves up, and Holly found her gun and ... I tighten my fingers on the edge of the rusted metal I'm hiding behind. I feel it bite into my skin. They got her. They actually killed her. And now it's like I power down completely and slump to the ground. Tina's dead. I can't get beyond that. For a minute, two minutes – I don't know how long – I just kneel there in the dirt unable to think or say or do anything.

So it's just me.

And now I'm so overcome with grief and loneliness, I get this terrible urge to just stand up and come out. 'Here I am. Take me away, lock me up. I'll tell you what happened but you won't believe me. And it doesn't matter anyway, because in a few hours, we're all toast.' Maybe those creatures are already out, maybe they've already started killing people. Maybe ... no. *Stop*. I can't go there. Not yet.

I turn and squint out into the smoke. Two cops are standing in the yard by the yellow trucks. I can hear the fizz of a radio but I can't hear what's being said. Next thing there's a blinding flash, and a bang almost straight after. The fire must have reached another cache of ammonium nitrate. The two cops spin away from the blast and run, crouching, back towards the car. The flames intensify, washing the yard in orange light, and I do a double take. The boot of the cop car. It's open. It's hard to see in the smoke, but I'm nearly certain it wasn't open a second ago. Is that movement? In the shadows at the back of the ambulance?

The two cops are standing right there, twenty metres away, directly between me and the car.

Another flicker in the shadows. There she is! There she is! Tina, flattened against the back of the ambulance. The cops are only a couple of metres away from her, standing just this side of the car. Next thing one of them turns and sees the open boot. He says something to his colleague and now everything about them changes. Suddenly they're super alert, looking around, squinting into the smoke. One of them stares right into the shadows where I'm hiding. Tina, still at the rear doors of the ambulance, is edging towards the corner, about to stick her head out. *No!* I'm thinking. *Stop! Stop! Go back!* The two cops move to the front of the ambulance. Now that their backs are to me, I step out and start waving my arms. She doesn't see me. When the first cop yanks open the ambulance's driver's door, Tina, still hiding at the back doors, starts and ducks down. The other cop has gone around the front to the other side of the ambulance and is opening the passenger door. He pulls out a torch; I see its beam flash across the smoky air. Both of us, me and Tina, realise at the same time that the next thing they're going to do is go to the back of the ambulance, so what does she do? She gets down and rolls under it, so that her head disappears, then reappears right beside the back wheel.

Cop #2 now appears at the back of the ambulance. My bag in one hand, the bolt cutters in the other. The bolt cutters with the label 'Property of David Ryan' in neat white letters down along the handle. *Oh God.*

When he opens the rear doors of the ambulance, the cop's face is screened from view. The other one is still standing at the driver's door, his back to me. So I step out again and wave frantically at Tina, and this time she sees me. She sees me. And I know by her that she thought I was gone or dead or something too. But there's no time to celebrate. She starts pointing frantically at the cop car, at the back of the cop car which is just to the right in front of her. And she's doing something weird with her hands and mouthing something that, in the dancing light of the fire, I can't make out. I shrug and do a big *What?* gesture, and she repeats the charade. Then I get it. She's made guns of her fingers and is pointing at the boot. She wants us to steal the cops' guns, which she reckons are in the boot, which is now closed again. She must have managed to get it open before but clearly didn't have time to get the guns out. If there even are guns in there. Do cops keep guns in the boots of their cars? Tina can tell from the look on my face that I've figured out what she wants to do. Stealing cops' guns. If I had my phone, I'd take it out and look up what kind of sentence that carries. What do we want guns for? We've got the explosives.

But the cops are all over the ambulance. In half a second, one of them is going to shine his torch underneath it and she'll be caught. Now, she's pointing down the yard towards the fire. Yeah, I know, I know. We need to distract them, get them away from the ambulance, away from the car.

By now the fire has spread to the trees and is getting brighter and louder, crackling and roaring and lighting up the sky.

The quarry trucks. Eight of them, all in a row. I swallow hard and pick the one furthest away. I zero in on the bumper jutting out, zero in and think it forward. Nothing happens for a moment, then I see it – the bumper – tear from the front of the truck, fly into the air, then drop into the burning prefabs. The cops don't notice. The fire has drowned out the noise it must have made when it ripped from the truck.

Tina makes a *Come on!* gesture, and I make an *I'm doing my best* gesture. Both cops are now rifling through stuff inside the ambulance and I can see it rock a little from their weight.

This time I stare hard at the front of the truck, but I think the whole thing out. I imagine it moving slowly forward, towards the fire, towards the cops. And I know it's working because I can feel that pain flicker awake at the base of my skull. And now here it comes. The truck edges out along the concrete. The brakes are on so the front wheels aren't turning, and over the roar of the fire, there's a high-pitched squeal that brings the cops springing from the back of the ambulance. With my mind, I drag the truck out further, then push it, push it down towards the back of the yard, away from the fire, away from the ambulance and the car, away from us. Running now, the cops call out. I hear them speak for the first time.

'Stop! Stop there!'

And I almost do, but I don't. I push the truck down along the concrete, feeling the pain creep up the back of my head, feeling it push its fingers in deeper and deeper, and I grit my teeth against it. Tina breaks cover before I do. When I see her edging towards the cop car, I stop pushing the truck, but the headache doesn't stop. It only stops getting worse. I stumble-run from under the quarry machinery to the ambulance, my eyes on the backs of the two cops running towards the truck. Tina dives into the front of the cop car, finds the lever for the boot and flips it. I grab my bag and the bolt cutters from where the first cop dropped them. I throw them into the back of the ambulance and ease the door closed.

Then I make it to the passenger door of the ambulance and climb in. Tina appears on the driver's side, her face black with smoke, her eyes bright.

'No bloody guns,' she says.

'Good.'

She climbs in.

I can only see one of the cops. He's climbing up the side of the cab of the truck I moved, trying to open the door. The other one must be doing the same on the other side.

'Time to go,' says Tina, and in two seconds we're back out on the road and Tina is accelerating away from the quarry and the cops, past the burning trees, back towards the village and the mines.

'Dunvilles'?' I say.

'Yeah, Dunvilles'.'

12. C#

By now, Tina seems to have got the hang of driving. There's not half so much jerking or gear-grinding. She takes us by the back roads to Dunvilles', which has been our rainy-day bolt-hole for years. It's this ruined mansion that sits at the end of a long sweeping avenue on the Lisard Road. A hundred years ago, it belonged to the Dunville family, along with pretty much everything else in and around the village. They're long gone and the house is in ruins.

The ambulance rumbles up the potholed avenue and the house is suddenly there, huge and shadowy. I bring up the map of the mines on Tina's phone and together we trace the route we took from the pit-head in Maher's field down to the chamber where we found Mam and Dad. I now realise how far we travelled underground and how close to the sea we came. The problem is that there's no other open mineshaft anywhere in the village. None. Which means we'll have to go back to Maher's to get into the mine. The slight problem there is that, even if everyone's gone home, it's now blocked by about a thousand tons of rock and earth.

I start to say all this, but Tina zooms in even further. 'There was another tunnel out, remember? In the place with the eggs. There was a second tunnel out the other side.'

She's right. There was.

'Look, what's that?' she says, taking the phone from me. She points to the faintest line running right to the edge of the screen.

'It's a dead end – it goes out to sea,' I say.

And now Tina breathes in sharply. 'The stack.'

'The stack?'

'The mine runs out as far as the Brenner Stack,' she says, 'and the stack is hollow. That's how we get in.'

Now I remember what she's remembered. Last year some time. Before the fall. Enda lives across the road from the cliffs and the Brenner Stack. He brought us out there, to the stack. He said he wanted to show us something.

'It only works,' he said, 'when the wind is exactly south by south-east.'

I remember tramping over the hummocky field opposite his house, with the sheep scattering in front of us and the wind rushing in over the edge of the cliff.

A few metres from the edge, he called back to us. 'Hear that?'

A note. A deep hollow note. Blowing on and off. It was hard to tell where it was coming from.

'It's C sharp!' said Enda, grinning and pushing his glasses up his nose.

'What is it?' I asked.

'What does it sound like?' he replied.

'It's like … someone blowing across the top of a bottle,' says Tina.

'Exactly! It's the stack. The stack is hollow, or at least there's a pit-head out there. An open pit-head. A way down into the mines.'

'No way.'

'Got to be. It's the only explanation.'

Now, sitting in the ambulance, Tina looks at me expectantly. I know exactly what she's thinking.

'I'm not sure I can get us out there, Tina.'

'Me neither. But do you have any better ideas?'

Oh God.

When we get up near the ribbon of houses where Enda lives, I get out and open the gate into the field opposite. It's small and stony and ends abruptly at the cliff edge. Tina turns the ambulance in to the field and begins weaving between the rocks and furze bushes. I shut the gate after us and she pulls up a few yards back from the edge. She kills the lights. When she climbs out, we stand there for a minute in the darkness, listening. We can hear the sea now, hissing and sucking way down below us. It's too dark to see the stack.

There's a feeding trough in the far corner of the field. It's like a big black plastic bath divided into two sections, both full of water. It takes the two of us to haul it from the concrete blocks it's sitting on, empty it out and drag it back to the ambulance. We fill one side of the trough with all of the explosive stuff, then stand there looking at it. The night is so calm – it's like it's got no idea what it's in for.

Neither of us wants to take the next step. What if I kill us both? What if I set off the explosives by mistake? The thought of having nothing but fifty metres of empty air beneath me …

'Shut up, brain.'

'What?' says Tina.

I climb into the other side of the feeding trough and hunker down, stuffing my backpack under my knees. Tina suddenly thinks of something and disappears into the back of the ambulance. Minutes later, she's back, carrying a big grey bag with wires trailing out of it.

'Is that –?'

'Defibrillator,' she says. 'Need a charge to trigger the explosion.' She lowers it into the plastic trough alongside me as her phone starts ringing again. It's been going almost non-stop over the last half an hour or so. This time she pulls it out.

'Mam,' she says. 'Eight missed calls.'

I don't say anything but I watch her stare at it. She puts it on silent, shoves it back into her pocket and looks down at me scrunched up in my side of the trough.

'If you kill me,' she says, 'I'm going to come back and haunt you.' She can't keep the shake out of her voice.

It's like the pain is waiting just offstage. As soon as I start to concentrate on the trough, a dull ache pings the base of my skull. We're right at the edge of the cliff, closer to it than I would ever come in real life. But this isn't real life. This is an endless chain of exhaustion and terror and exhaustion and terror and so on and so forth.

I zoom in on the scuffed black plastic and just, sort of, well, think it up. And just like that we're up and rising, lifting smoothly and far too quickly from the ground. I panic and think, *Hang on*. Well, I don't mean to think it, but I do, and the feeding trough sort of judders in the air and one of the bags of ammonium nitrate slides off the pile down on top of us. Tina gasps and grabs the sides more tightly. I zoom in again on the trough and just sort of hold it, with my mind. I hold it in mid-air, maybe a metre and a half off the ground. I hold it just for a second and then move. Not towards the cliff edge, not yet. I move smoothly forward and higher. The pain holds steady at the base of my skull. It's manageable, it's ignorable, but it's there and I can tell it's only beginning. Tina's breath is coming fast.

'It's OK, T, we're doing OK. I'm going to circle the ambulance, just to make sure I can control this.'

As I say it, we drift rapidly towards the ambulance and pass smoothly around it. I repeat the exercise, but slightly higher this time, almost at the same height as the ambulance roof. Then I pause and move straight up. Higher and higher. Tina makes a small noise, and I know she's biting back a bigger one. Now we're, I don't know, fifteen metres above the ground? Oh God! It's only a few days since I clung to the ladder, three metres up, putting up those trail cams. And the ridiculousness of what I'm doing hits me like a bucket of ice water. I'm sitting in a feeding trough fifteen metres in the air with nothing – nothing at all – holding me there. The trough drops.

'MARTIN!'

I zero in once more on the trough and think, *Wait!* and we decelerate rapidly, so that we're pushed down into our side of the trough and another bag slides off the pile on top of us. We hang there, panting like dogs.

From the corner of my eye, I see a car coming up the coast road and, beyond that, the twinkling lights of the village. The pain at the base of my skull intensifies. There's no ignoring it now. Better get this over with.

I think us lower, slowly, and we drop through the air gently, but not gently enough. The last half a metre or so happens too quickly and the trough hits the ground with a painful jolt.

'Sorry.'

We get out, put the fallen bags back on the pile and tie them all in place with the rope from my backpack, then we both climb back in.

'OK,' I say, 'this time for real.'

There's a war going on in my head. I need to concentrate in order to fly, which is hard to do when most of my brain is screaming that what I'm attempting is impossible and will result in violent death. And now, the pain is weighing in too. Creeping up behind my ears, spreading into the back of my head. I dig the bike light out of my backpack and hand it to Tina; then we squeeze back into the trough. 'Ready?'

'No.'

'Me neither.'

I clench my teeth, and we rise smoothly off the ground, then drift right to the edge. I hold there for a few seconds. Then I inch out a little further so that the far end of the trough is above the sea. Then a little more, then a little more. Tina's got the bike light in one hand, shining it out into the darkness. When we're about half out and half not out, I swallow a howl and just go – and then we're just gone, flying out into a beam of murky light, with nothing below us but fifty metres of air. We're moving quickly, a little more quickly than I think I want, and for half a second that unease drives out every other thought. We lurch lower sickeningly. Tina cries out – her body is like a wound spring behind me – and then, with a big inward breath, I'm back in control. We're moving up and out, a little more slowly, a little more evenly. Now the bike light picks out the bleached bulk of the stack away to the left. We adjust and move towards it. But the pain. It's spread down into my shoulders and I'm afraid it'll take over. I feel dog-tired and regret I tried that test flight back at the ambulance. But we're coming closer and closer. It's hard to judge height. I don't want to go too low and hit the side of the stack, or too high and have too far to drop. Now it's there, right beside us, and I slow and shift a little higher so that it's directly beneath us, or at least I think it is. Sweat is hot and sticky on my skin, and I'm easing lower and lower, until I think it's just beneath us. I can't be sure, but I think us down, inch by inch.

'A little lower,' Tina whispers.

So I go lower, lower, lower. And now there's resistance. A soft sponginess. We're here, we've landed. But we're not level. There's a slope. It's not steep but I hadn't expected it. From the cliffs, that little cap of grass had always seemed flat. We're slipping, slipping towards the edge. I know I need to stop it with my mind, I know I do, but I can't. In the darkness I can't seem to distinguish between the trough and the ground, and the pain is making it harder to zero in on it.

'Get out!' I shout, and we both scramble out, then try to grab the trough before everything slides over the edge. But it's heavy, and now that it's moving and I'm panicking, I can't seem to stop it by just thinking about it. I've no energy left. My ears are ringing and my eyes want to close. Tina grabs the trough but doesn't have a good grip and I'm afraid she'll go over with it.

'Let it go!' I grab her, her grasp fails, the trough full of explosives slides off into the darkness, and Tina screams in frustration.

13. BANG

Game Over.

I slump down on the grass. After the weightlessness of the flight, I now feel like I weigh about four tons. My arms and legs are jelly.

'You've got to see this, Martin.' Tina's voice – she's not going nuts. She's panting and panicky, but she's not going nuts.

'What? What is it?'

'He was right. Enda was right.'

So I turn over and grab two fistfuls of the rubbery grass. Have to be super careful. We're stranded on a tiny platform with a fifty-metre fall one false move away. I drag myself down the little slope to where she's crouched, shining the bike light down onto the grass. Except it's not grass at all. It's a hole. A dark rectangular hole rimmed with scraggly yellow weeds.

'Did the trough go down there?' I ask.

'Yep.'

'And the stuff didn't blow up?'

'Nah,' says Tina. 'Have to set the charges. And look.' She reaches further into the blackness with the light. Steel rungs, just like in the pit-head in Maher's field.

We hover there, listening, but there's nothing to hear.

'We've lost the element of surprise,' I say.

'Who cares?' she says, then roars down into the hole. 'Ready or not, here we come!'

The climb down is nearly as scary as the flight. My arms are so wobbly, they feel like they belong to someone else, and it takes me ages to reach the bottom. But it's nothing like as deep as Maher's, and the base of the pit, when it comes, doesn't take me by surprise. I can see one of the burst bags of nitrate just below me. It looks like salt scattered everywhere.

The area is narrow and sort of circular, with one tunnel leading back towards the shore. The other bags have landed in a pile, with the defibrillator on top; this doesn't seem to have broken. Two of the bags have burst and the trough has split lengthways and is in two pieces.

Tina shines the light into the passageway. It's narrow and leads downwards. The light glitters on the water collected there and I hear a steady *drip drip drip*.

She piles the nitrate bags onto a broken section of the trough so we can drag them to the chamber – assuming that's what's at the end of the tunnel. I find the shopping bag and gather up the charges. A few are in pieces but most are OK.

This tunnel is much narrower than any we've been down before now. The timber supports are further apart and the rock walls are much more uneven. We've hardly gone a few metres when it gets even narrower.

We have to go sideways through shallow water and can only manage one bag each. The super-narrow section goes on and on. It's horrible. It squeezes my chest, and I have to stoop to keep from hitting the ceiling.

We find the first one just after this section.

For a minute I think it's just rock. It's got uneven ridges running along the top, but when I put my hand on it, it feels steel hard, not rock hard. And warm. For a moment I'm confused, we both are. Tina runs her hands across the top of the thing. Nearly three metres long and a metre high. Pointed at one end.

It's a chrysalis, an insect case. Has to be. There's got to be a pupa developing inside it. But it's so much bigger than I thought it would be, way bigger than the maggots were. I mean you could fit loads of them inside it.

'This is not good,' says Tina.

She takes the hammer from the side pocket of my backpack. When she brings it down hard on one of the ridges, there's a loud clang, like a gong being struck, and a spark flies off into the darkness. She does this three times before we bend to inspect the damage. There's no damage.

This is not good.

The next one is a little further along the passage, then we come on two, one on top of the other. Then there are three and it's another tight squeeze to get past. When we get into the chamber where we found my parents, the place is packed with them. How many? I don't know, it's hard to tell. Hundreds maybe? Stuck to the walls and ceiling. Piled so high we can hardly get through. Each one is held in place with a yellowish mesh. This looks soft to the touch, but is every bit as solid as the cases themselves. When Tina strikes at it with the hammer, it rebounds without leaving a scratch on the case.

This is not good.

For the next half an hour or so, we go back and forth through the narrow tunnel, bringing the surviving bags through one at a time. Then I dig the penknife out of my bag and hand it to Tina. She slits the first of the nitrate bags down the side. 'Spread it around,' she says, 'get it into all the little gaps.'

I'm wrecked. I got the flu last year and spent three days lying on my back, barely able to move. That's what it feels like. I've been running on adrenaline for the past few hours, but now that needle's edging towards empty. This is pointless. I've never been more sure of anything. Our chance was when they were larvae. Now they're transforming into something horrible in those long, unbreakable tubes. This is not going to work.

Tina's darting about the chamber with the light, carrying nitrate on a broken piece of feeding trough, packing it into crevices and gaps. If she knows this is pointless, she's not letting on, she's not giving in. But soon now, very soon, all of this manic stuff will have to end and both of us will just collapse somewhere and wait for the end, whatever form it's going to take.

She must sense me looking at her because she says, without looking up, 'Am I supposed to prevent the apocalypse on my own or what?'

She sets out these red candle-like things and blasting caps like she's been doing it all her life. I don't bother asking her to explain what's going on. What's the point? Then she begins threading the thin yellow wire through the blasting caps. We train it back up the passage way. I try to help, but really it's all Tina. I barely have the energy to drag myself along.

At the base of the pit, she takes out the penknife again and starts stripping back the ends of the wire.

'Get that,' she says, nodding towards the defibrillator.

I haul it over. When she has both wires stripped, she wraps the exposed copper wire round and round the defibrillator paddles, then hits the green button on the machine.

'This is it,' she says. Her voice is calm. 'Hold onto your hat.'

'Maybe we should climb back up, T.'

'Do you want to be on the top of the stack when it gets blown up?'

'No, but I don't want to be at the bottom either.'

She shrugs and looks at me, really looks.

I shrug back.

We both hunch down on the damp floor of the tunnel, ready to get into crash positions. I clamp my hands around my ears. Tina wraps one hand awkwardly around her head, to try to cover both ears, then she looks at me again, and again she shrugs.

She hits the 'shock' button on the defibrillator.

It's like someone hits pause and the planet stops turning. For a second I think it's failed. Then it comes. The explosion. It's everywhere at once – in the sea, in the shaft, in the rock. The whole stack seems to shudder and there's a sound of rock splitting and grinding against itself. Curled up on the floor of the tunnel, I hear a whoosh and feel a rush of warm air. When I open my eyes, I can't see anything. Nothing. But I can hear water rushing in. Is this how it's going to end? Trapped and drowned in rising water?

Tina pulls me to my feet.

I know she's got the light on, I can make out a glimmer just beside me, but the smoke has doubled up the darkness, and it's so thick, I know if I try to breathe in, I'll choke, so I duck down again – we both do – and breathe through our teeth. I can still hear water coming in, but it's not coming in here – it must be somewhere further down the tunnel. The stack hasn't collapsed, so we're not trapped, not yet anyway. We stay hunched in the darkness for, I don't know, ten minutes or something, waiting for the smoke to settle.

'We're still alive,' I whisper.

'Yeah, well,' says Tina, 'don't get used to it.'

When we eventually stand up, she runs the bike light slowly around the cavern. It's as if it's been sprayed with thick black paint. Soot covers everything: our clothes, our hair, the backs of my hands. I can feel it clinging like grease to the back of my neck.

The first timber frame right at the entrance to the tunnel has partially collapsed, but it looks like it's still possible to climb through into the passage beyond. There's a lot more water underfoot, and I can still hear it rushing in somewhere up ahead of us. We pick our way down along the passage until we get to the place where it narrows. Here, the way is half blocked by fallen rock, and here's where the water is coming in, squirting through a hole overhead. This place is going to be completely flooded very soon.

But we keep going. Tina climbs over the fallen rock, then slides down the other side into the passageway beyond. I hear her gasp.

'What is it?'

'Water.'

I follow her in, and sink to my chest in freezing salty water. But worse than that is the narrowness of the passage. I turn sideways to get through and feel the rock close around me like a fist. The air is rotten. Hot and full of smoke, so bad we both start coughing.

Then we come to the first case, partially submerged in water. It's just as we left it. Apart from a thick coat of soot, it's intact. It hasn't even moved. We say nothing but struggle through to the chamber, passing half a dozen others; all fine, all perfect. In the chamber itself, where Tina concentrated most of the explosives, the water is knee-deep.

Everything is black, and one side of the chamber has collapsed completely. There they are, hundreds of them, held in place with that unyielding yellowish mesh. Not a scratch.

Game over.

14. SONG

All the adrenaline is gone now. There's no need to rush any more. When we get back to the base of the ladder, I let her go up first, but when it's my turn, I can barely manage it. The only thing that gets me out of there is the fact that it's so dark and stuffy and wet and smelly and horrible. I focus on each rung as I meet it. One hand, one foot, one hand, one foot, as if they're the only things in the world. I try to stave off the truth, which is circling me like a bird of prey. *You're just picking a nicer place to die.*

Eventually, we're back on top of the stack, lying on the grass, staring up at the sky. I'm so exhausted, I could sleep here. If it wasn't for what we're about to face, I probably would.

The moon is up now. It's three-quarters gone but there's still light from it. Not that I'm looking, not that I'm doing anything but lying here, panting.

Tina pulls out her phone and takes it off silent. It starts buzzing with messages and notifications.

'The cops have been to my house. Mam is mad. Her texts are all in caps.'

'Call the hospital, T, will you? See if my parents have woken up.'

She finds the number and gets through quickly enough; then she hands me the phone.

'This is Martin Ryan. My parents were brought in earlier. Can you give me an update on them?'

When the receptionist tells me to wait, her voice is bored, but when she comes back a few minutes later, she's like my best friend.

'Your parents are in a stable condition, Martin, but they haven't woken up yet. Now, the gardaí are here and want to –'

I hit the red button. 'They're still out.'

'So that's it then,' says Tina.

I don't answer. After a while, I say, 'I don't think I can get us back, T.'

'I know.'

Silence.

Then she says, 'At least we don't have to worry about exams any more.'

'Oh yeah, never thought of that.'

'No homework.'

'Or beans on toast.'

We both hate beans on toast.

'Monday mornings.'

'Nuclear war.'

'Imagine. In a few years, New York will be all over-grown. Like in that film. And London.'

'Everywhere.'

Silence.

Then Tina says, 'You remember when Enda asked us if we thought we were lucky?'

He used to come up with questions like this all the time. *Where would you go if you could time travel? What would be your super power?* Odd questions too, like, *Do you think your parents are happy? What would you do if you found out you were terminally ill?* We used to spend hours talking about the possibilities.

'I remember.'

I said I felt lucky. Tina wasn't sure about herself, but Enda, he said that you never really know if luck is good or bad. Something bad happens, like you break your leg. But the following week you don't walk out in front of the car that would have killed you.

'*Where would you spend your last hours on Earth?*' she says. 'He asked us that, you remember?'

'Oh yeah.'

'You remember what he said?'

'A laundry. He said a laundry.'

'He loved the smell of laundries. He said he'd make a big nest of all the clean sheets.'

Silence.

'I'd never have thought of it,' she says, 'but the three of us on top of the Brenner Stack, that'd be pretty cool.'

'Too high for me.'

Silence.

'You were right,' she says eventually.

'What?'

'I did run away, after Enda fell. You were right.'

'Tina, it doesn't matter. I don't –'

'It's weird,' she says, cutting across me. 'If you'd asked me before it happened if I'd ever do anything like that, I'd have said no, no way, not in a million years. But I saw him fall, and I, and I heard him cry out. Did you hear that? The way his voice sounded?'

She glances at me and I shake my head. I don't remember that at all.

'I looked down and saw him there, on that ledge. And he was dead, I was sure of it. So I ran. I didn't decide to run. I didn't think about anything. One minute I was there, the next I was on the bike, pedalling away from there as fast as I could. It wasn't that I felt guilty or blamed myself or anything. It's, like, I don't know. I think about this all the time and I just can't believe I did it. But I did do it. I just kept pedalling as hard as I could until I was exhausted and couldn't go any further. Then I stopped the first car that came along and got a lift back. And all the time, you were there, halfway down the cliff, keeping him alive.'

'It doesn't matter, T.'

'It's all I dream about now,' she says. 'It's all I've dreamed about since then. Him falling. Almost every night. Over and over and over again.'

Silence.

'I miss him the way he was,' I say. 'I miss him so much.' Putting this into words for the first time, hearing my own voice say these words to her. It's unbearable.

'Me too,' she says, so quietly I can hardly hear her.

Silence.

'He was coming back too,' I say. 'I mean, I'm not saying he was going to be like he was, but ...'

I feel her nodding next to me.

'You think he might have come up with a better idea?' I ask. 'You think he could have got us out of this?'

'He was good.' Her voice is small. 'I don't think he was that good.'

Silence. Then Tina's breathing changes.

'Tina –'

'I smashed that thing, the signal thing. I ruined everything.'

'Stop, you didn't –'

'I did, it's all my fault.'

'Tina, stop.'

'It is, though, Martin, it is.'

'Tina, it's not your fault Billy and Holly are homicidal lunatics.'

But she's not hearing me any more. She's panting, she can barely speak. 'I'm the reason the entire human race is going to be killed.'

'Stop! Stop it!' I sit up. 'What more could we have done, Tina? We collapsed a mine, and stole an ambulance, and blew up a quarry and a mine ... and ... that signal thing mightn't even have worked. Half of Dad's schemes don't come off.'

And now her breathing is all shaky and fast. She sits up. 'I don't want to die, Martin.'

And I can't say anything; my voice won't work. I just reach out my hand. She takes it and she squeezes so hard it hurts. I swallow and try to get my voice under control.

I start singing our song, only not really singing, more speaking, but my voice is so shaky that it just sounds daft, so she snorts out a laugh, except it's more of a sob, but I keep going. She joins in then, and it's the lousiest version of the song you've ever heard, but we get louder and louder until we're singing at the tops of our voices.

There's a very loud sound from the pit. A crack, echoing upwards. We go still. Another crack. Then a horrible sound, like giant hands taking a sheet of metal and tearing it down the middle.

We look at each other, but her face is so frightened I can't hold her gaze. Instead I just look down, at the rubbery grass, at the darkness, at anything other than her face. My mind is stuck in a terrible loop. *This is it, this is it, this is it, this is it, this is it, this is it, this is it.*

I see Tina turn her head and look into the darkness below us. I know what she's going to say next. But she doesn't say it. She looks at me and nods and we both stand up. I don't want to have to see those things from Holly's hologram. I don't want to see them. And I don't want Tina to see them. I don't want them to be the last thing she sees. I reach out for her hand.

Then her phone starts ringing. She glances at the screen, then does a double take.

'What?'

'Enda.'

'What?'

'It's Enda.'

Enda hasn't used his phone since the fall. Enda can't use his phone. He's not capable of using his phone. Tina hits the green button and brings it up to her ear. 'Hello?'

I lean in but I can't hear anything.

'Hello?'

Next thing there's music – it's a bit faint at first, like it's playing on a tiny radio with the volume turned most of the way down. Then it gets louder and there's no mistaking it. Twisted Sister. 'We're Not Gonna Take it.' I look at Tina, utterly bewildered. The song plays on for another half a minute, then the line goes dead.

'It's his phone,' she says. 'It's his old number.'

'How?'

'You know where his phone was? I do. It was in my bedroom. It was in a box under my bed.'

She calls the number back

'What was it doing there?'

'I took it. After the fall. I know it was stupid, but I just wanted to have something that belonged to him before – before he fell, before he hit his head. No-one knew where that phone was, Martin, no-one. And no-one knew I took it but him. That day, the day I took it, we were in his room, me and him, and I held it up and I said something like, "I'm taking this." And he didn't make any sign that he heard me or understood me or anything, so I just took it. And it was dead. It was dead, Martin. Somehow, he went to my house, he got the phone, he charged it, he put credit on it and he rang.'

The phone rings on and on, but no-one answers.

'Maybe it's a trick, maybe they –'

'No, Martin, no, it's not a trick. He's the only one who knew I took it. This is him telling us "I'm back." This is him saying, "Don't jump, I've got something."'

'What? What has he got?'

'I don't know! Something.'

'Hang on. Two days ago you refused to believe that he had matched two cards. Now you think he's found a way to defeat an army of mutant alien insects and save the human race?'

'Oh God, keep up, Martin. He's getting better, I get it. You were right. I was wrong. OK? Happy? Now you've got to get over there.'

'What?'

She grabs me by the shoulders. 'I know you can't bring me with you. I know you can't. That's fine. I'll stay here. You go.'

'No way, Tina.'

'Martin.'

'I'm not leaving you here.'

'Martin, listen to me. This isn't about you. This isn't about me. This is the chance. This is the only chance. You've got to go find him. It's simple.'

'Tina, we don't know for sure that –'

'No, we don't. But what's the alternative? Jump. Die.'

'Tina, I –'

'No, Martin, no. It's shut-up time.'

I'm thinking frantically.

'Get up on my back,' I say.

'No.'

'Can't we just try?'

'If you could see yourself, Martin. You're half dead. You're pale as a ghost. If you carry me, we might get halfway over, then we'd fall, and then whatever Enda has is useless.'

'Tina.'

'Shut up. This is a lifeline, Martin. For everybody. For your parents, for Mam, for my little nieces and nephews and … We can't risk it. You know that, you can see that too.'

Another crack and a tearing sound from the pit.

'I ran once before,' she says, standing back. The fear is gone out of her eyes. 'I'm not running again. I'm just not.'

'Tina.'

'Go. Now.'

Next thing I know, we're hugging. I don't know which of us started it, but we're holding each other so tight, it's almost like we're wrestling. Then she stands back.

'Tina, I –'

'Martin, I swear, I swear, if you don't go, I'm going to push you off.'

She takes a step back and braces herself and I know she's serious.

'Don't jump, Tina, OK?'

She won't answer.

'Promise me you won't jump.'

'Just go!'

Next thing I'm up, hovering above the stack. And I'm off, over the sea, my eyes fixed on the lights of Enda's house, my body feeling like I died and it's just my ghost flying towards the cliffs.

15. TRAINS

When the door opens, it doesn't open the whole way, and it takes me a minute to recognise Enda's granny in a pink dressing gown. I've no idea what time it is, but it must be late, probably very late, and I must look terrible – caked in soot, soaking wet and barely able to stand.

'Hi, it's me, Martin, Enda's friend? I know it's late, sorry. Is he in?'

'Who is it?'

I remember that she's a bit deaf. 'Martin, Martin Ryan? I'm Enda's friend.'

She stares at me for half an hour or something before she opens the door. 'Come on in, Martin, come in. Are you all right? What are you doing out at this hour? God, I didn't know who it was. You're soaking, so you are. Are you all right? You'll have a cup of tea.'

She ushers me into the kitchen.

'Sorry, I'm in a bit of a rush. Is Enda here?'

She talks over her shoulder as she fills the kettle. 'Sure aren't his parents out looking for him. He hasn't been home since this morning. They're combing the countryside, out of their minds with worry. This getting-lost business must be a bit contagious, I'm thinking, between yourself and the young O'Reilly girl and now Enda.'

'He's missing?' I move towards the front door. 'He's in my house, he's at the trains.'

'Hold your horses there now,' she says. 'Didn't they check there first? Of course they did, but hide nor hair of him could they find. They've half the road out looking for him.'

As she talks, one of Enda's sisters appears in the hall doorway just behind her granny. Ciara. She's also in her dressing gown and is holding a finger to her lips. She points towards the back door and mouths something – I don't know what. She disappears.

'Now, hang on there a minute, Martin Ryan, I have something for you. I just have to nip down the hall.'

Enda's granny pulls out a chair and more or less pushes me down into it. 'You just sit down there now and I'll be back in a minute. Will you do that? Will you sit down? Just for a minute?'

She doesn't wait for an answer but goes back out into the hall. I head straight for the back door.

The garden is full of trees which block out the moonlight.

'Ciara?'

There's a light moving rapidly back and forth somewhere ahead of me. I move towards it.

'Ciara! Come on,' I hiss. 'I don't have time for this. Do you know where Enda is?'

The light disappears for a moment, then reappears, moving to and fro about six metres from the ground.

Enda's dad built a house into a big ash tree at the bottom of the garden and nailed a ladder of timber struts for the girls to climb. More rungs. Great. The second I get my arms onto the platform which forms the floor of the treehouse, a light is shone into my eyes.

'Password!' says one of the girls.

'Come on! There's no time. Do you know where Enda is?'

'PASSWORD!'

I can't see anything with the light in my eyes, but now the other girl is at my shoulder.

'It's "Krakatoa Split Terracotta Blanch",' she whispers.

'Oh for God's sake.'

'Password or you shall not pass!' says the first one and pinches my nose.

'Krakatoa split terracotta blanch!'

The light pulls back. 'Enter, friend.'

I clamber up and find Ciara sitting cross-legged on the floor. Saoirse is hanging the head torch she's been holding from an overhead hook. There's an upturned milk crate in front of them with a pillowcase draped over it.

'Granny May isn't like other grannies,' says Ciara. 'She's kind of horrible.'

'She's always taking out her false teeth and chasing me with them,' says Saoirse, who looks just like Enda.

'Look, that's terrible, but I don't have time for this. Do you know where Enda is?'

'It's relevant,' says Ciara, 'because, as we speak, she is calling the cops on you.'

'What?'

'They were over earlier. Tina stole an ambulance, and they know you're in on it.'

'What?'

'Yeah, Robin,' Saoirse adds. 'She's clearly the brains of the outfit. You'd never think of robbing an ambulance.'

'The cops were here?'

'Are you deaf?' says Ciara.

'Look, OK, thanks for the tip-off. I have to go.' I turn round.

'Enda's not as broken as everyone thinks. Not any more,' Ciara says. 'He can't do what he used to be able to do, but he can do other things.'

I stop and turn back to them.

'You can't talk to him in the old way,' says Saoirse, 'but you can talk to him, sort of.'

'He hears everything, he understands everything,' says Ciara. 'It's just hard for him to make you understand what he wants to say.'

I look from one to the other. 'How does he talk to you? Does he use the cards?'

'OK!' says Ciara, blinking. 'So you're not a complete moron.'

'I knew it! I knew he was trying to tell us stuff.'

The older one points to the upturned crate. 'Show him the thing.'

Saoirse pulls the pillowcase away, revealing two bananas and a drawing, a childish drawing of, I think, a house.

'We're not sure,' says Saoirse, 'but we think we have to give these to you. That's what we think he wanted us to do.'

'Like I say,' says Ciara, 'it's not easy to figure out what he wants.'

'He's not missing?'

'He is but he wants to be. We think he wants you to find him.'

'Bananas and ...' I pick up the drawing, 'this.' It's a house all right. Big and square with a triangular roof. Something lumpy and round in the doorway. An animal? A sheep maybe? There are lots of crooked windows and what may be another sheep overhead. Or is it a cloud? The little marks that streak the sky could be rain. It looks like someone started to draw trees around it, then got bored and gave up.

'Enda drew this?'

'Yes.'

I stare at it. 'Dunvilles',' I say. 'It's Dunvilles'. That's where he is.' I turn to go down.

'Take the bananas,' says Saoirse.

'What? Why?'

'He obviously wanted you to eat them.' Ciara is talking slowly, like I'm a slow on the uptake.

'Fine.' I grab them.

'No. Eat them. Now.'

'I'm not hungry.'

They stare at me.

'God. Fine. OK.' The second I tear back the skin, I remember. 'Bird, Boy, Banana.' Ciara looks at me sharply. I go on. 'Those are the three cards he always goes for.'

She nods. 'They're not the only ones, but yeah, he uses them a lot. We think boy is you; bird, we don't know. We're pretty sure banana is banana.'

'Why?'

They shrug in unison.

'Hang on,' says Ciara. 'Do you know what the bird is?'

Bird. Flight? Could he really have known? Could he? I shake my head. Through mouthfuls of banana, I ask them if they have a bike I could borrow.

'Enda's old one is against the back wall,' says Ciara. 'Figured you'd need it.'

'Brilliant. Oh, and can I have that torch? Please?' The bike light is back with Tina on the stack.

Ciara unhooks the head torch and hands it over. I climb down as fast as I can. As I run across the garden towards the back wall, Saoirse calls out. 'Good luck, Robin!'

The bike is old and too small, but it'll do. I take off down the road and look out towards the sea stack, but at this distance it's too dark to see, even with the moon out.

The police are out looking for us. If what Ciara and Saoirse say is true, that Granny May really was calling them on me, then chances are they're on their way up the coast road. So I'm whizzing down the hill with the head torch switched off, scanning the ditches ahead of me for the light that's going to tell me there's a car coming towards me. The mudguard is rubbing off the back wheel of the bike and the chain rattles. I can't hear over the noise, so the light is all I'll have to go on. And it comes eventually. I squeeze the brakes, but of course they don't work so well, so I have to drag my foot along the road to slow down, then I toss the bike into one ditch and wade as quickly as I can into the opposite one. It's briars and mud and water, but I scrunch down into it as the car comes speeding up the hill. It is the cops. There's no screaming siren or spinning blue light, but the streak of white and blue and yellow is unmistakable. They're driving so fast! I mean, dangerously fast. We're in so much trouble. God.

I wasn't spotted, that's the main thing, and the car continues on up the road towards Enda's without slowing down.

I'm back on the bike as soon as they're gone, and I know I need to get off the coast road fast because those cops will be back. So I turn off at the first opportunity and pedal furiously along the back roads as far as Dunvilles' without meeting another car.

It's so quiet and so dark when I get there that for the first time since I recognised the drawing in the tree house, I wonder if it's just a wild goose chase. What if he's not here? What if there's nothing here but the big, dead, empty house? Worse, what if he is here but he's got nothing, and it's just us in the darkness and Tina trapped on the stack and those things about to come and get her?

I use the head torch to pick my way round to the back of the house. This is how we always get in.

'Enda?' I call quietly, but there's no response. So I clamber over the rubble piled against the back wall and climb through the window to get into the narrow corridor that leads to the kitchen.

Light. I see flickering light.

'Enda?'

I round the corner into the kitchen. It's candles. Ten or more candles sitting on shelves and on the rickety table. Enda's on the floor, his back to me, surrounded by … I'm not sure what it is at first, but there's a familiarity about it.

It's trains.

It's bits of Dad's train set. My heart sinks. It's just the trains. It's nothing. It's Enda and the bloody trains.

'Enda.'

He's sitting on the floor, working at something I can't see. He's breathing heavily through his nose. I walk round but he doesn't look up. It's like I'm not even there.

'Enda!'

He's trying to fix a length of rail to the side of something, to one of the model-train shelters. The shelter is made of brown plastic, or at least I always assumed it was. I mean, I never thought about it. But the underside of it is covered in – is that circuitry? Electronic circuitry? Enda is trying to insert the section of rail into something at the base of the shelter, but he's having trouble making his hands do what they're told. I bend down and, taking his hands in mine, I guide the prongs of the rail into a socket in the shelter. A socket that shouldn't be there, a socket that makes no sense. There's a kechunk sound, a satisfying kechunk sound, and light rushes through the circuits. I breathe out and Enda looks up, looks into my eyes, directly into my eyes.

'What is this?' I ask him.

As he straightens up, I see that what he's just made is only a part of something bigger, something with a lot of interlocking parts, about the size of a vacuum cleaner. A series of curved rails fixed to sockets at the base of the shelter link into another set of sockets in a grey power unit. The last time I saw this, it was fixed to the wall of Dad's shed. The power cable is looped round and round the steeple of the model church, which is fixed via another set of rails to a section of the viaduct that was the centrepiece of the whole set. A length of curled flex extends from this to something else that lies in shadow on the floor. Enda picks it up. It's one of the engines from the train set, a diesel engine. He takes this and guides it into another socket in one of the arches of the viaduct. When he does, the whole thing comes to life. There's a beeping sound and lights rush from one end to another. The way he cradles it, it looks like … I mean it's a …

16. MARIO

Enda stands up suddenly. Then I hear it. A car. We both go still. It's not out on the road. I wish it was, but I know it can't be. The house is so far from the road that if a car was to pass by, there's no way we could hear it in here. The car is driving towards us; it's coming down the avenue. It's so close that I can hear it rocking over the tractor ruts that make the narrow road so bumpy. Then it's at the front of the house, then the side. No-one could have any business here at this time of night. It can only be the cops.

Enda stands there silently, cradling the thing he's built, while I rush around quenching the candles. The smell of smoke fills the kitchen and I know then that there's no point in hiding, in hoping they'll find the place empty and go away. They'll be in here in a couple of minutes with flashlights. I switch off the head torch. We stand there in the pitch darkness, waiting. For a moment I don't hear anything; then there are echoing voices and footsteps towards the front door. I grab Enda's elbow and flick my own light back on. Then, moving as quickly and as quietly as I can, I guide him back down the dusty corridor to the back window. I climb out and try to take the thing from his arms so that he can follow me, but he won't give it up. As he rolls awkwardly through the window, a booming male voice calls out, 'Hello! Come out, come on out now!'

The man's tone is so commanding that I stop dead for a moment. It's like my whole body wants to do what he says, but Enda keeps moving. He passes me by, and before I can stop him, he's clear of the rubble piled against the back of the house. I don't call out to him, I can't risk it. I figure he'll head for the fields, the wide open space behind the house, but he doesn't. He heads down along the back of the house, towards the corner.

'No!' I whisper as loud as I can. 'Enda!'

The cop car is just around this corner. I can hear the engine running and see the headlights blazing out across the ditches and dilapidated walls at the back of the house. If Enda steps out from behind the back wall, he'll be seen. I scuttle after him, but he can move fast when he wants to and he rounds the corner before I can stop him. I stick close to the back wall and when I reach the end, I poke my head out slowly. There it is, the cop car. Both front doors open, engine running, lights on full. No cops. They must both have gone in through the front door.

Enda is climbing into the passenger seat.

'What are you doing?' I hiss at him, darting over. 'Enda, come on! We can't do this.' I try to pull him out, but he's immovable. He's sitting there holding the thing he's built, staring dead ahead. 'Enda, come on! I can't drive!'

He's like someone's granddad, waiting to be taken out for Sunday lunch. I glance behind me, expecting the cops to rush out and pin me to the ground or shoot me or something. 'Enda! Please!'

What can I do? I close his door gently, then rush round, dive into the driver's seat and pull the door closed. The seat is about half a mile from the steering wheel. So I sit on the edge, grab the wheel and … now what? I look down at the pedals. There are two. Shouldn't there be three? Where's the gear stick? There's no gear stick, just a lever where the handbrake should be. It's an automatic. An automatic. No gears. OK, fine, that's good, that will make it easier. I need to go backwards. A three-point turn so I can drive forward out the gate.

Bam! Someone's at the window. I hit the door lock a split second before the handle is pulled. It's a cop, a great big enormous cop, so big and enormous and angry, I can't actually look at him.

'Open this door immediately, Martin.'

He knows who I am. Oh God, oh God, oh God.

'I'm really sorry about this, but I can't. Sorry. Really sorry. Sorry, sorry, sorry.'

'You are committing a very grave offence, Martin.'

'I know, I know, it's terrible, I'm really sorry.'

I pull the lever back so that it clicks into the 'R' position and push my foot down hard on what I hope is the accelerator. The car jerks back across the uneven ground far too quickly, then there's a hollow bang and we stop dead. The other cop is at Enda's window, hammering on it and roaring at us to open the door.

'Oh God, oh God, oh God, oh God, oh God.'

I move the lever out of reverse, turn the key and the engine jerks to life again. We lurch forward with a tinkling of glass. I fiddle with the steering wheel and the side of the car grinds painfully along the pillar, so I spin it the other way – narrowly missing the opposite ditch – before straightening up and accelerating down the avenue. I glance in the rear-view mirror, but I can't see the cops. We're moving too fast now; there's no way they could keep up on foot.

By the time we get to the road, bits of the car – I'm thinking probably the bumper – are hanging off. I can hear them bobbling along behind us.

'This is crazy. This is nuts! How did this happen? And what even is that thing?'

Enda's sitting there, holding it, but now he turns to me, he actually turns in my direction. He's never done this, not since the fall, never given us the slightest indication that he was aware of what was going on.

He says a word. A full, clear word.

'Gun.'

It's the first word I've heard him speak in nearly ten months.

'A gun! Oh my God, Enda. You talked. Oh my God.'

This distraction sends me sliding across the road, so I whip the wheel back, but too much and nearly end up in the opposite ditch again.

'This is crap. I'm no good at *Mario Kart*. I've never been any good at it. I'm *Minecraft*. *Minecraft* is my game.'

So now I try to keep the thing in the middle of the road, grateful that it's so late and there are no other cars about.

It only takes five minutes to get back up the coast road. The gate into the field where we parked the ambulance is still closed, but I don't bother to get out and open it. The car is in bits anyway, and I'm going to jail for the rest of my life one way or another, so I just accelerate into the gate and it springs back violently. The car leaps and bucks over the bumpy ground, throwing us around. I keep going, past the ambulance, until we're a few metres from the cliff edge. Then I clamp both feet on the brake and pull the lever back until the car jerks to a stop. I jump out. The wall of the stack glows white in the cop car's headlights. I can't see the top.

'Tina!' I call, then hold my breath, listening.

Nothing. Not a sound, just the hiss of the sea down below us and the rustle of the grass and reeds in the field. I call a second time, squinting into the darkness, but I can't see or hear her.

There's a sound behind me. Enda is climbing out of the car, still cradling the thing he built. In the darkness I can't see him properly, but I see blue light flare along the edges of the device. Then he pulls the trigger – I mean, I assume that's what happens – because a bolt of blue light, the size and shape of a biro, shoots up out into the sky with an electric *fizzt*.

It's a gun; it really is a gun. A sophisticated alien weapon Dad had been hiding in among the trains. Of course he had a weapon. He, of all people, had to be prepared. Of course he had a weapon.

There's another *fizzt*, and another shot of blue light flies out and hits the door of the cop car with a sound like a sledgehammer hitting a radiator. The car disappears. I mean it *disappears*. Not just the door. The whole thing. Completely.

'Oh God. I mean, it's great and all, but did you have to disappear the cop car?'

With the light gone, I can't see the stack at all. But now I hear the scream of a siren. Suddenly there's whirling blue light everywhere and two more cop cars come racing up the coast road, one directly behind the other. I pivot to watch them pass. If Enda hadn't zapped the one we stole, the headlights would have given us away. Did he know they were coming? Did he zap the car on purpose?

I wait until the cars vanish, then I roar again into the darkness. 'Tina!'

I get down on my stomach and wriggle to the edge of the cliff, sticking my head out, feeling the wind rush up into my face and willing the whole world to just shut up for a minute so I can listen.

Is it the wind? The sea? No, it's a voice. It's her, I'm sure of it, it's Tina. And she's in the water. That's where it's coming from. The sea.

'Oh God.'

Before I paralyse myself with any more questions, before my brain can get itself together to stop me, I get up, take a few steps backwards, then run and leap out into the darkness. And I fall and fall, with the wind howling around my ears. And I don't think anything for a moment – I'm just falling. And I just trust that I won't hit the water, that the fall will stop being a fall and become a flight. And I don't slow, I don't ease to a stop, the speed even seems to increase but the angle changes, and now I'm swooping, I'm not falling any more. I'm swooping until I'm shooting along the top of the water, my face inches from the surface.

This is when I realise that there's no pain. None. At all. Weird. Why is that? I've been bracing for it but it never arrives.

I spread out my arms and open my eyes wide and I slow down and rise slightly. Then I slow some more until I'm hovering there in the air, just above the churning sea.

'Tina!'

Nothing.

I'm off again, in a wide arc with the Bremmer Stack at its centre. Slowly, in a standing position. I'm trembling but there's no pain. None. I feel fine. Weird.

'Tina!'

And I know calling out is diverting my attention, but I'm not going to fall. I just know I'm not. I don't have to put any thought into it. Why would I fall? What would be the point of that? It's like gravity is an idiot calling me names. Why should I listen? Why should I pay it any attention? Why would I need to think about it?

'Tina!'

And I hear her. I'm not sure from where, but I hear her. So I move closer to the stack, then drift slowly in a narrow arc across the top of the sea.

'Keep shouting! I can't hear you!'

'Here! Here, you moron!'

17. ARMAGEDDON

She'd jumped off the stack just before Enda and I returned from Dunvilles'. Waiting up there, listening to those creatures breaking out of their cocoons was too much to bear.

'How are you still alive?' I ask her. 'Why don't you have hypothermia?'

'I don't know. I wasn't in there long enough I guess,' she says.

We're in the ambulance again. Enda's in the front, with me. Tina's in the back, drying off and changing into a fresh set of scrubs. That's the great thing about having an ambulance during Armageddon. There's all kinds of super-handy stuff in the back.

'I went down so deep,' she says. 'I just kept going and going, down and down. It took ages to get back to the surface.'

When she did, she swam to the little group of rocks on the shoreward side of the stack and dragged herself up onto them. That's where I found her.

'Did you see them, the insects?'

'They didn't come out.'

Enda has the gun on his lap. It's in two parts. There's a big chunky section, mostly made from the train controller unit, the model shelter and the model church.

This is connected via two wires to the firing part: the train engine is the barrel and the handle is a section of the viaduct. The trigger is a small gold-coloured switch that hangs from beneath the engine. I see now why he had to take everything to Dunvilles'. He needed time to assemble the gun. If he'd stayed in Dad's shed, his parents would have found him and taken him home.

My eyes keep going back to the dark bulk of the stack, which is a shade of deeper black against the grey-black of the sea. I keep thinking I see movement out there.

'So where are they?' I ask, as Tina climbs into the space between the front seats.

'I don't know. Still down there, I suppose. Wow. That's it? Enda, can I see?'

He uncurls his body and she carefully lifts the machine from his lap. Her hand closes around the barrel.

'Careful! He made a cop car disappear a minute ago with that thing.'

Resting the part with the control unit on her knees, she leans across Enda and aims out through the open door. But when she pulls the trigger, nothing happens. She fiddles with it and tries again but, as before, nothing happens. When she tries a third time, blue light flares briefly around the edges of the barrel and it beeps twice, but it's like a shutting-down signal.

'Gah! What's wrong?' she asks.

Enda makes a noise and she passes the device back to him. The instant his hand closes around the handle, there's a different set of electronic noises and the blue light travels around its edges again. It's powering up.

'It must be locked onto his fingerprints or something.'

'Maybe.' Tina glances at me, then does a double take. 'What happened to you?'

'What? Nothing.'

'You don't look like death any more.'

'Well, thank you.'

'No, dude, out there, before, you looked like you were going to die. You were white, I mean white, and your eyes were popping out of your head.'

She's right. I am feeling a whole lot better than I was the last time I went flying. Well, I'm exhausted and sick with fear, but I don't feel like my head is going to explode. My ears aren't ringing. In fact, there's no pain anywhere, and if I think back, it's been like that since, since, I don't know – Dunvilles'? Since Enda and I stole the cop car? Why?

Next thing, Enda makes another sound, and his arm comes out and moves shakily towards us. It's like it's being operated by a bad puppeteer. The hand jerks up and his fingers close on the keys dangling from the ambulance's ignition. He holds them for four or five seconds before letting go and curling back into the seat.

'Go?' says Tina. 'Go where?'

'If we go,' I say, 'the cops will get us. Shouldn't we stay here, wait for the insects to start coming out of the stack, then shoot them down?'

This whole time, I have my eyes fixed on that oblong hunk of darkness out in the sea, waiting for something awful to come flying out of it. It occurs to me, too, that if we're going to shoot down a hundred or more of these things, Enda probably isn't the right man to be holding the gun. I saw him trying to aim that thing at the cop car. Sure, he hit it, and yes, I know he intended to do it, and yeah, it helped, but God, it took so much effort – and the cop car was right there: I mean, it was easier to hit it than miss it. But a swarm of mutant alien insects? How's he going to aim at them?

'If they were going to come up through the stack,' says Tina, 'wouldn't they have shown up by now?'

'So Maher's field then? It's the only other opening.'

'They don't need an opening, though, do they? Billy said they can get through anything.'

And we both see it together.

'The village,' says Tina. 'They're going to drill up into the village. That's where most of the people are. Here, swap.'

I move out of the way, she climbs into the driver's seat, and I take up her perch between the two seats. She turns the ignition and the engine jumps to life.

The lights blaze out into the darkness, illuminating for a moment the top of the stack, before arcing away as Tina steers the ambulance back towards the gate. We blunder out over the fallen gate and turn on to the coast road.

Next thing the siren starts wailing and I jump. 'Tina! What did you do? We're supposed to be in stealth mode.'

'It's not me, moron!'

I spin round and see it through the back window. Not it. Them. Cop cars. Probably the same two that we saw speeding up the coast road earlier in the night. 'Just keep going, Tina, just keep going.'

'I know!'

If they're behind us, I'm thinking, they can't do any damage, they can't stop us, but the road widens just before the junction with the Glencooper road, where we have to turn down into the village. They'll be able to pass us then, and if they pass us, they'll be able to block us. They'll stop us, drag us out and that'll be that. So I turn and climb into the back of the ambulance.

'What are you going to do?'

'I don't know.'

The boxes that Tina had pulled out to find fresh clothes are sliding round back there. I stumble over them, then get thrown into the side as we go around a bend. I crawl to the back doors, drag myself up and grab one of the overhead straps. I undo the doors. They swing open suddenly. If I hadn't had a good grip on the strap, I'd have tumbled out. Two boxes of medical gear – bandages and stuff – shoot out onto the road and get crushed under the wheels of the leading cop car.

It's right there – I mean, right there: just, like, two metres behind us. So close that their headlights are shadowed by the back of the ambulance and I can see right into the car.

The driver is giving me the Look of Death. Beside him in the passenger seat there's a guy with a baseball cap pulled down over his eyes. I can clearly read the letters 'ERU' in yellow across the front of it. Emergency Response Unit. Then I realise he's holding a gun across his chest. Oh God.

'I'm really sorry about this!' I shout. 'It's not our fault, honestly!'

Tina roars back at me. 'What are you doing?'

The guy driving mouths something. I don't know what it is.

'Pardon?' And I hold my hand to my ear.

He gestures fiercely with his hand that we should pull in. The guy with the gun looks up. His face doesn't have any expression, but I can tell he's only dying to use it. The gun, like.

Oh God.

So I just start thinking about the car chasing us, not about the super-scary dudes driving it, just about the car and its wheels spinning so fast, eating up the road behind us. I think hard about them spinning and ... and then I just think about them spinning a bit slower ...

It's like the cop car hiccups. It jumps, and the two guys are thrown forward. Suddenly there's ten metres between us. So I lock onto those spinning wheels again, and I think about them slowing and slowing. The car lurches to the side again, and the two guys get thrown forward a second time. I can't see their faces any more: they're too far back and the headlights are too bright. And that's good because it's not half as hard to stop them if I'm not getting the Look of Death. So I stare at the place where the driver's side front wheel is, and I think about the air inside of it, pushing against the tyre. I'm dangling there from the hand strap, both doors flapping open, and I'm thinking about the air in that cop-car front tyre pushing and pushing and pushing against the rubber until pop! I think pop! but the sound is more like a gunshot, and for a second I think the ERU guy is after taking a shot at us, but it's not that. It's the tyre exploding.

'What's going on?' Tina roars.

I can see the car's headlights getting further and further away, but the other car is now edging around it, so I focus on the road behind us, and I'm imagining it ripping away, unpeeling like a banana, and then that's what happens. The surface rolls away, leaving rock and black dirt, and I think up and it explodes up into the air and now there's a big black crater in the middle of the road. Nothing is going to get past it.

Five minutes later we're in the village. We stop at the square. Tina kills the engine and she and I climb out. It's silent. I mean, dead silent. It must be two or three in the morning. The street lights are on, and the beer ad up on the wall of the pub – a guy with a moustache pulling a horse inside a cart – is lit up, but there's no light in any house.

The square is really a triangle, just beyond the beach car park. Three roads lead from it. The Glencooper road we've just travelled down. The school road and the church road lead uphill with the little park between them. Not really a park, just a couple of benches and some flower beds surrounded by a low wall. Tina takes the school road, I take the church road. We don't leave each other's sight; we move slowly, turning around, watching, listening. There's a bit of a wind moving between the houses, but other than that, there's nothing to hear.

'Maybe they've all malfunctioned,' I say when we get back to the ambulance. 'Maybe they're all, I don't know … stuck underground and can't get out.'

She doesn't answer, just stands there in the half-light, mouth ajar, listening. Enda's in the cab, sitting back now in the seat, gazing upwards. There's a muffled *fzzt* and the glass in the windscreen is gone. Not just the glass. The roof of the cab, the doors and the frame around the window are all gone and Enda is sitting there, rigid, staring up the school road. He makes a noise, like clearing his throat, and we're both up beside him in a second.

'Up the school road, yeah?' Tina turns on the engine and Enda makes the same noise.

'Oak Tree Heights,' I say.

This is an estate at the top of the hill. There must be sixty or seventy houses there. Probably the most densely populated area in the whole place. We speed up the road, skid in through the entrance and screech to a halt. I jump down. 'Turn off the engine.'

The engine goes quiet, but, but it feels like it hasn't. The sound dies but I can still feel vibrations through my feet.

It's like there's a train approaching, but the nearest railway tracks are thirty kilometres or more away. And now there's a sound too. For a minute I can't make out whether it's near and quiet or far away and loud. And then it feels like it is coming from everywhere at once. Louder and louder. The vibrations intensify. Then they're not just vibrations. The ground is shaking. This is what an earthquake must feel like.

It's happening.

18. TURTLE

Tina jumps down from the ambulance but the shaking ground knocks her forward. All around us, car alarms start to scream. Lights come on in houses. The look on Enda's face is … Well, it's the old Enda, the pre-fall Enda. He's concentrating intensely, his eyes wide. The ambulance is rocking on its wheels.

Then the first one breaches. Six metres from us the earth rips open, filling the air with dust and bits of soil and rock and clumps of broken tarmac. The thing shoots clear into the air. It's a nightmare of legs and claws, wings a blur. Hovering there. Turning with fast, jerky movements. And big, so big. Much bigger than I had expected.

Fzzt! A blue bolt shoots from the cab, catches its thorax and it's gone. Just gone.

Enda. *Enda* did that.

'Yeah!' Tina roars. 'Die screaming!'

In the next second, three more giant bugs erupt through the hole the first one made. They don't hover like the last one did. The first dives towards us, I scrabble backwards. I don't see or hear the blue light from Enda's gun, but it must have come because the thing is gone.

The other two bugs make straight for the nearest house, darting with that weird stop-motion speed and making a noise like a low, rumbling buzz that I can feel in my stomach. It's like they move from one spot to the next instantaneously, without passing through the space in between. They're halfway between a mosquito and a scorpion. But so terribly big, with long segmented bodies and folded narrow legs. A curled tail topped with a barb. And claws. Each one the size of a car.

Enda's bolts of blue light flash out, but this time, he misses. He's still in the cab of the ambulance, but turned at an awkward angle. I can see he's having trouble controlling his arm. It's wobbling – it won't do what it's told. That intense concentration is still on his face. His forehead glistens with sweat. I dash back to the ambulance. I know there's no point in trying to take the thing from him, but I take his arm. I aim, he fires.

Fzzt! Got one.

Fzzt! The blue bolt of light shoots off into the sky.

Fzzt! Got the other one.

Tina jumps back in the cab, turns on the engine and backs up. Yeah, this can work. She drives, Enda fires, I help him aim. This can work. This can work.

Now people are appearing in their front doors. Dressing gowns and jumpers thrown on over pyjamas. I don't think anyone's seen any of the bugs we just vaporised. They're staring at us and the crater in the middle of the entrance to their estate.

'Get back in! Get inside!' Tina is yelling at them from the cab, but everyone is in full-on stare mode, too bewildered and too curious to do anything else.

What happens next happens far too quickly. The back of the ambulance rises suddenly. For a second I think it's going to do a full somersault and we're going to be tipped out and crushed under it, but instead it jerks to the left and Tina and I are thrown on top of Enda. The ambulance teeters horribly; then it crashes onto its side. Another bug has come up behind us. Without saying anything, we both seize Enda and half drag, half push him from the wreck. He hasn't let go of the zapper. I mean, he didn't even try to protect his head as he fell. He's still locked in that same pose: one arm holding the section with the power unit, the other on the handle of the weapon. He raises this as we haul him out and the fzzt! is right in my ear. I can tell from the sound behind me that he got one that was about to attack. I spin onto my back, grabbing his arm. Five, six, seven bugs rush upwards into the sky. The dust is thick, but I aim as well as I can. *Fzzt! Fzzt! Fzzt! Fzzt! Fzzt! Fzzt!* Most of the bolts of light flare harmlessly into the sky. Only two of the seven disappear.

'Here, you do this,' I call to Tina. 'Shooters are your thing.'

Enda is propped against the fallen ambulance. He's exhausted: he can't keep this up. Tina crouches beside him and takes his limp arm exactly as I did. She aims, Enda works the trigger. One by one they pick off the last five. As they do, I feel the ground rumbling and I know that what we've seen so far is just the beginning.

The doorsteps are deserted now. Car alarms are still blaring and there are lights in windows. I run deeper into the estate, turning around, looking for something, but not sure what that something is. There's nothing we can use, nothing except … except …

I grab the thing, tip out the water and drag it back to Tina and Enda just as another crater opens up alongside the first. Dust and rock and chunks of broken concrete are flung up into the air. A huge boulder smashes down into the side of the fallen ambulance and a fresh wave of bugs rises up into the sky. Tina and Enda fire into them. She's doing better than I did, no doubt, but now there are so many, and they get so far so quickly, that it's almost impossible to get them all.

'Here! Get in!'

Tina turns and sees me standing in front of an empty paddling pool in the shape of a turtle. It's yellow with purple spots.

'What? What for?'

'We've got to go after them. There's nothing else to use.'

'OK,' she says, nodding. 'Cool.'

Enda doesn't resist. He climbs in and crouches down. Tina arranges herself behind him, then reaches forward and takes the arm that still holds the gun. There's not much space but I get in behind them.

'Hold on.'

I clutch both sides and think us up. And that's what happens. I think us up and we rise, evenly and probably a little too fast, into the sky. There are no seat belts, obviously. The sides of the thing are only, like, half a metre high.

The best we can do to stop falling out is to push our feet against the sides and kind of brace ourselves in.

'Don't kill us, Martin.' That's all Tina says before she turns again to the bugs.

Then they explode from the ground, one after the other like a jet of water. I pull us up and back, trying to give Tina a good angle to aim from, while at the same time keeping the turtle parallel to the ground. Not easy. The gun can only fire so fast, but they're doing well, Enda and Tina. Most of the shots are hitting home and the beasties disappear before they know what's going on.

'Bring us lower!' Tina shouts, and I see straight away what she wants. If we can just keep the gun on the hole as they come out, and maybe shoot down into it, we can hit them before they have a chance to get out of the way. Fish in a barrel. I ease lower, still trying to keep the thing level, but then the game changes. The flow of bugs from the hole intensifies, so that now there's two at a time shooting up into the sky. Next thing the earth cracks further into the estate and another geyser of war bugs erupts. I turn and see them stream in tight formation up into the darkness. There's a sound like a mountain being torn apart, a third hole opens in the earth, and another column of bugs shoots upwards, this one down at the back of the estate. Before we can draw breath there are twenty hovering in the air, turning jerkily, choosing targets. Now that there are so many, the buzzing is deafening, like dozens of bulldozers in the sky.

Some of them are going to get away. We can't let this happen. We can't.

'I'm going to try and get in closer,' I shout over the screaming alarms and buzzing wings. I don't even know if Tina can hear me. If we, if we … I don't know … swoop? And I think it, I picture the turtle, I picture it swinging down from the first crater to the second, then upwards towards the last one.

'Hold on!'

Fast, I think. *Fast*. And the swoop begins, and it's like a roller coaster, where you turn into a dive and you hold on and close your eyes and try to trust the restraint holding you in. Except there's no restraint. There's only my two hands gripping the sides of the turtle. Tina and Enda can't even do that. I lean back, trying to wrap my legs around Tina, and as we speed up, I can feel her slowly rise from the bottom of the paddling pool, and I don't realise I'm screaming till I hear it, but Tina doesn't seem to notice. It's like she's back in the little arcade beside Russo's in the village, her eyes fixed on the screen, like she's the only person in the world. *Fzzt! Fzzt! Fzzt! Fzzt! Fzzt! Fzzt! Fzzt! Fzzt!* The little bolts of blue light smash into the first wave of bugs, then into the next, then into the third. We come up out of the dive, I feel gravity push Tina and Enda back down into the turtle, then we arc round the third crater and turn into another dive, sending bolt after bolt of lethal blue light into them.

This time, I can hardly keep us all in the turtle. We're, I don't know, ten metres above the ground, and I feel them beginning to lift up and away from me. The only thing I can do to keep them from flying out is to go higher, so I do: I lift us up out of the dive and swoop up and away from the bugs.

Then it's like they notice us for the first time.

They all pivot in the air and come hurtling towards us from three different directions, and there's just no way I can –

'BACKWARDS!' Tina screams.

As they zero in on us, I reverse. I think, *Back, fast*, and keep thinking it. Still clutching the sides, I turn my head to see where we're going. We're down over the village – I think. The street lights have gone out for some reason, but I can make out the dark curve of the beach down to my left. This is what I head for while the three streams of war bugs swoop towards us. Tina and Enda fire straight into them, but for every row they destroy, another bursts forward to take its place. If I could just get out over the sea, I could skim along the top without having to turn my head backwards to watch for obstacles. We could move faster, we could –

'Martin!'

I turn back and see that the bugs have given up. They've turned and are climbing upwards in a huge column. Moonlight glitters off their grey-green bodies as they stream vertically into the sky. They've given up – they know we can destroy them. It's our turn to chase *them*.

So I think, *Up, up, up*, and we rise, so fast we're all pressed down into the bottom of the turtle, and I know I need to be careful here. If we stop too rapidly, we'll all be catapulted out, but I'm not stopping yet, because the bugs seem to be speeding up, and there's no sign of them changing course. They're still travelling vertically and we're high now, much higher than we've ever been, and it's much windier. Tina is aiming shots into them, and hitting the odd one, but they're too far ahead. *Faster*, I think, *faster*. And the speed is just mad now, the wind like a giant hand pressing down into the turtle. All the air leaves my lungs, but we're gaining on them, and Tina and Enda are still shooting wave after wave of blue light into them.

Then they're not.

'What's wrong?' I roar over the wind.

'Enda,' Tina rasps at him, 'you're not firing. Fire, now!' Only then we see that he is, his finger is still tight on the trigger, but there's nothing coming out. 'Enda! Do something.'

Overhead, the line of bugs is turning, finally, it's flattening out. I can see them travelling in a curving chain. How many now? Fifty? Sixty?

But we're so high. I don't want to check, I don't want to turn my head, to look down, I don't want to know how high we are. The wind is so strong, it's roaring in our ears, making my eyes water.

I can see that Enda is struggling with the machine. His right hand is still clamped on the handle of the gun. He's trying to move his left hand towards the red power dial on the controller. It gets halfway but then the wind takes it and his whole arm flaps backwards like a scarf and slaps me in the face.

'The dial, Tina! Let go his arm and turn the dial.'

When I look up again towards the line of bugs, I can't see them – I can't see them anywhere. Tina and Enda are busy with the zapper, and I'm pivoting in the constricted little space, trying to see where they've gone. Movement, off to the right. My stomach lurches. They've doubled back. They've doubled back and are accelerating towards us from the side. They're less than a hundred metres away and are coming straight at us. Only, something's wrong, it's not all of them, it's not all of them. I twist around. Another column coming in from the left. They weren't running at all: they're smarter than that.

'TINA!'

'I can't get it to work!'

'LOOK!'

I turn the turtle, first one way, then the other. I feel her body jerk backwards in fright. Then she's back frantically fighting with the controller.

'TINA!

'I KNOW!'

Closer and closer now, I see the one at the front of the left-hand column clench its claws and bring them together so that its huge body is like a missile thundering towards us.

I don't hear it but I see it. A beautiful bolt of blue light. It's working. She's got it working again.

'SPIN!' says Tina.

So I do. The turtle starts whirling in the air and the killing blue light spits out in all directions. Faster and faster. I clench my teeth, trying to keep that thought going: *Spin, spin, spin,* but in seconds I'm dizzy and disorientated. Squinting, I can see their blurred shapes barrelling towards us, closer and closer, so that, in seconds, the bolts of blue light strike home just metres from us. This goes on and on, and then I shut my eyes tight to drive out every other thought but that. *Spin, spin, spin.* Beside me, I can hear Tina roaring over the wind howling around us. But it's not roaring – it's words. 'STOP! STOP!'

I stop spinning, but it's like my brain doesn't. I don't know where I am; I can feel nothing but the wind and for a moment can't tell up from down. The turtle wobbles in the sky, then lurches lower and pivots downwards, so that for half a second we're all sliding out. We're screwed, we're done for. They'll get us for sure. Tina screams and I jerk the turtle back so that we're level again. But the bugs aren't there. I'm pivoting again, trying to see where they've gone, but between the dizziness and the wind, I can see nothing but blurred darkness.

'There!'

I follow Tina's arm and just about see them, swimming into and out of focus. A chain of them, like before, moving higher and higher. Way fewer now, *way* fewer. This time they really are going. We can't let a single one get away. We can't.

Fast, I think, *fast*, and we're gone again, upwards this time. I've got to keep the angle shallow so that we gain height without tipping out. But the wind. The wind just wants to swipe us out of the sky. It's like it hates us, like it knows we've no business up here. I want to move my hand to wipe the tears out of my eyes, but I can't let go, so I can only see if I squint. And now I see it too. I can't avoid it. The sea below us. We're so high, we're so high I can actually see the curvature of the Earth. But there's no land, only endless grey-black sea, way, way, way below us and gravity only dying to smash us into it.

But we're still too far away, we're still going too slow, so, *Faster, faster, faster, faster*, and it happens; we speed up, but my breathing is short and shallow now. The air is thin up here. Not enough oxygen. Won't be able to stay up here for long. Now I can feel the familiar pain rising up from the base of my skull. I don't know why it went away earlier, any more than I know why it's just come back.

Nearer and nearer. Close enough now for a shot. The first bolt of blue light arcs past the chain of bugs, but Tina corrects her aim and the next shot vanishes one of them, and so does the one after. I gulp down a mouthful of air and think, *Faster, faster, faster, faster*. The angle and the speed press Tina and Enda back into my chest, making breathing even harder. The blue lights ping through the darkness. How is Tina even aiming any more? How can she see? How can either of them breathe? There's only a handful of bugs left: six, seven?

But they seem to be able to move more quickly now. *Faster, faster, faster*. The pain spreads out, pushing itself deeper into my brain. And even if I could breathe in, there's no air up here. And I can't see anything any more. I'm gasping for air but my chest won't move, it just won't move, and my brain starts to tingle and …

19. FALL

This is it, the second fall. The first was just Enda, but this one is all three of us. I don't know this, not now, not yet. There's nothing only blackness. It's like deep, deep sleep. Like a chunk of time cut off and thrown away.

And then I'm back in the world. Or not in the world, really. Hurtling rapidly towards it. I blink and see the huge dark sea, then I don't see it, then I see it again, glittering and grey in the moonlight, coming closer and closer. I'm spinning and falling and falling and spinning. There's no sign of the turtle anywhere. But there's something beside me, something stuck to me – it's clinging to my hair. Over the roar of the wind in my ears, I hear a voice screaming.

'Wake up, you dozy moron! Wake up!' Tina has one hand clamped in my hair and the pair of us are whirling and falling and whirling and falling. 'WAKE UP!'

'Did you get them? Did you get them all?'

'YES!'

Slow, I think, *slow, slow, slow*. And the spinning slows and the falling slows, but the pressure on my head doesn't, because Tina is still whirling and falling and clinging to my hair like grim death.

I reach out and try to pull her onto my back. I try to think about us both slowing and not falling. I reach out my arms and pull her towards me and she grabs at my shoulder.

'My back.' It's hard to make my voice heard over the howling wind. 'Get on my back!'

'LOOK!' She drags herself towards me but doesn't let go of my head. She yanks it round so I see the dark figure below us, dropping and dropping.

Enda.

And I'm gone. Shooting downwards. It's instinct now, not thought. Tina's behind me, clinging awkwardly to my shoulders. We don't have time for her to get a better grip.

Closer and closer to the sea now. I know if he hits it at the rate he's falling, that will be it. No more Enda. So fast now I can feel the skin on my face being pulled backwards. The wind rushing past is deafening. *Faster, faster, faster.* Closer and closer. We've only got seconds. *Faster, faster.* My arms stretch out towards him. His body is splayed out by the wind; he's not conscious. I'm about to collide with him, and I try to think, *Slower, slower,* and feel Tina's body on my back become heavier, but I've slowed too soon and he drops further from me, so I dart forward and slam into him. The sea is everywhere now, I can hear it and smell it. I clamp my arms around him, tight as I can and now: *Slower, slower, slower.* Tina is a dead weight behind me and Enda is a dead weight in front of me, and it's all I can do to hold onto him.

Tina is roaring something. 'SLOW DOWN! SLOW DOWN!'

And then the sea gets us.

20. THREE MONTHS LATER

I've placed the phone under my pillow and set the alarm to vibrate at 2.15 am, but I'm up before it even goes off. I haven't really slept at all. I slip out of bed, go silently out into the hall, then to my parents' door. I wait there, listening to their breathing, until I'm sure they're both asleep, then I come back to my room, get dressed and slide my backpack out from under the bed. The fourth and seventh steps creak, so I avoid these as I edge down the stairs. Once outside, I collect my bike from where I've left it at the side of the house.

The moon is bright. No need for lights. Nothing on the road. I'm up at the field opposite Enda's house in less than ten minutes. I heave the bike over the wall. Then I climb over and pick my way carefully through the field. It was raining earlier and the grass is slick and damp. Overhead, there's a big bank of cloud moving towards the moon, and the wind brings the usual salty sting. It's cold but I'm well wrapped up. A few metres from the edge, I unpack the blanket, double it over, spread it on the grass and sit down. There's the stack, standing out there in the dark like always. The sea is sucking and splashing and glittering, but when the moon disappears behind the cloud, it becomes nothing but a big emptiness way down below me.

I'm early. I'm always early.

Eventually I hear sounds back at the gate and turn to see a grey shape climbing over it. I take the torch out, turn it on and hold it high, moving it back and forth so she can see where I am.

'Hey.'

'Hey.'

She sits down beside me on the blanket.

'This week any better?' she asks.

'Not really.'

'It is pretty funny, though.'

So it turns out that there was a dash cam on the cop car that Enda and I stole and drove from Dunvilles' up to the cliffs. Before he zapped it and made it disappear, footage from that trip got uploaded to the cops' central server, and they used it as evidence against us. Afterwards, it got leaked online. It's got, like, a million hits. You can't see me, you can only see the road, but the soundtrack is me, freaking out and apologising to the things I keep hitting and going on to Enda that I was never any good at driving games. It's like the funniest thing that anyone's ever seen.

'Not doing my street cred any good,' I say.

'Dude, you were never cool.'

Everywhere I go, there's this constant tittering. People point and laugh and don't even try to hide it. I never thought I'd miss the old days when I was invisible.

***

Not long after we hit the water, we found the yellow turtle again and used it to keep ourselves afloat. I was so exhausted that I couldn't do anything but cling to the side of it and try, with Tina, to keep Enda's face out of the water. We were found eventually, after I don't know how long. I remember the trawler pulling us out and I remember the rattle of the engine and the cries of the gulls as we headed back to shore, but I don't remember the ambulance that met us at the quay, or the hospital. I woke up with Mam, in a dressing gown, standing over me. She was holding herself up by the drip-stand that was still hooked up to her arm. She was smiling and crying at the same time.

'Is Dad OK?'

She nodded. Then I saw the cop standing by the window with his arms folded, and I knew that none of it had been a dream.

My parents had been on the point of telling me. All about who I was and where we came from and the rest of it. They had it all planned for my birthday. They have scrapbooks and pictures of my grandparents and relations and the place they come from. I haven't even looked at those yet. One thing at a time.

'We made nothing up, Martin,' Mam says. 'We just had to change our stories around a little. We did lie, but we lied as little as possible.'

I get it. I get it. I get it. I can see why they did what they did.

But.

It's as if the world and everyone in it was a blur before now, only I hadn't realised it was a blur, not until someone handed me a pair of glasses and said, 'Here, this is what it *really* looks like.'

So there's an invisible security ring all around Earth. Nothing is supposed to get through. In the past, there have been breaches by non-humans, but in the last couple of decades, the biggest threat to Earth is from humans. Billy and Holly aren't the only ones upset about what we've done to the planet. They found a weakness and smuggled all those stolen eggs into the mines. And, like I guessed, it's no coincidence Mam and Dad were posted here, to Glencooper. There are sentinels at different points all over the planet. About a hundred and sixty in all. They're usually sent to remote places or places with old mines or cave systems where awful things like those bugs can be hidden easily. That page I found in Dad's office? It was his mine inspection schedule.

Being a sentinel is a lifetime posting. Most sentinels are couples who do exactly what Mam and Dad did. Move here, set up some sort of life and then just, well, live it. And if something bad starts happening, break out Signal 87 and call in the cavalry.

We've had these long talks where they basically replace all of the lies in my head with the truth, and fill me in on all of the things they felt they couldn't tell me before.

We were at the kitchen table, with the remains of dinner growing cold and the sun going down behind the trees outside.

Dad said, 'We weren't supposed to have any sort of weaponry, Martin.'

'But we do keep up to date on what's happening politically,' said Mam. 'Again, we're not really supposed to. We're supposed to forget about our old lives, but it's easier said than done. And as we've gotten older, I think it's fair to say we're not as trusting as we used to be.'

'I know how you feel.'

Dad looked away and Mam looked hurt, but she nodded.

'Sorry,' I said.

'You have a right to be angry, Martin,' she said, and tears started in her eyes again. 'And when I think of what you went through …'

'It's OK. It's OK.'

'Back home,' said Dad, 'I was a weapons engineer. I retrained when I came here, but, to be honest, I didn't feel safe without some sort of protection, so I took parts from the ship and designed and built a new –'

'The ship?'

'Yes.' I followed Dad's gaze out through the window.

'The shed?' I said. And they both nodded.

'How?'

'Well, it's more or less decommissioned now. It was really only designed for one-way travel. I know, you'd think it would be sleek and aerodynamic, but – well, wind resistance isn't an issue in interstellar travel, so a thing can look like whatever you want it to look like on the outside.'

'Right,' I said, staring at our weather-beaten garden shed, which looked like a million other weather-beaten garden sheds, and I realised that it kind of makes sense. If you're Doc Brown, you build a time machine into a DeLorean, but if you're David Ryan, you build a space-ship into a garden shed and you disguise a weapon as a train set.

'I obviously assembled and disassembled the dee-mat around Enda so often that – sorry.' He held up his hands. 'The weapon. It's a dematerialiser. Dee-mat for short. It's pretty cool, if I say so myself.'

'A dematerialiser?'

As he talked, other little pieces of history slid into place. He used to get a magazine about guns in the post a few years back, and he reads books about military history. He was a weapons engineer. Imagine.

'So the whole obsession with trains, that was just … pretend?'

Dad looked shocked. 'Good lord, no. The rail network is fascinating. Railway engineering is probably the most –'

Now I held up my hands. 'OK, OK. You like trains.'

Mam said, 'Enda obviously watched your dad take the thing apart and put it back together so often that he remembered how to do it when he needed to.'

'That's what he was doing in there? Watching you take that apart and put it back together again the whole time?'

Mam and Dad looked at each other.

'Now what?'

'Not the whole time,' said Mam. 'We've also been working with Enda. I've been working with him. We can't bring dead brain cells back to life, but we can speed up the process of neural regeneration. This is where you encourage the development of new neural pathways when old ones are closed off because cells have died. This is cutting-edge stuff here, but it's quite routine back home.'

She stumbled a little saying 'back home'. Covering things up for so long is a hard habit to break.

'In the shed?'

She stood up. 'Come on. We'll show you.'

It was like some kind of magic trick. The door opened and instead of the huge table with its miniature landscape, its roads and bridges and train tracks and buildings and tiny people, there was empty space. The room was large and high-ceilinged and white and clean as a laboratory. The light felt like sunlight, but there were no windows, and when I turned back and looked out through the door, there was just the dusky dimness of the garden. It was the walls, it was as if they were giving out light.

'It's a kind of cloaking technology,' Dad said. 'Part optical illusion, part simple mechanics.'

He did something with his hand and two panels appeared in outline on the wall, then slid back to reveal what looked like tools, neatly arrayed in racks. A bench slid with a whisper from the wall, a row of tiny Perspex drawers filled with components beneath it.

I turned around slowly, taking it all in. 'I was here before, wasn't I? That time with my appendix.'

My mother nodded slowly. 'You remember that?'

'A little. It's like this when Enda's here?'

'Some of the time, yes. I have equipment here, medical equipment that I've been using. It's a slow process, neural stimulation, but it's working.'

'He'll be back to normal?'

She nodded. 'Yes. I think so. Speech, well, communication in general, involves diffuse parts of the brain working together and will take longer to come back. But I think you've seen how sharp his senses have become.'

I nodded.

Just after we arrived at the cliffs in the stolen cop car, the first thing Enda did was zap the cop car, making it disappear before it could be seen by the other two cop cars tearing up the road. He knew they were coming. And he figured out about the bananas too. Mam and Dad were always eating bananas. Always. Turns out they have just the right mix of heavy metals and trace elements to prevent what Mam calls TTH. Telekinesis Tension Headache. If Enda's sisters hadn't insisted that I eat them, there's no way I'd have been able to make it back out to pick Tina up, and no way in the world I'd have been able for the Battle of the Turtle, which is what we call it now. Eventually, the banana effect wore off, which is why the headache came back in the end, but by then it was nearly over.

***

'Biscuits?' says Tina.

I dig in the bag and take out a packet of Custard Creams and a packet of Viscounts. She rips open the Custard Creams and shoves two in her mouth.

'So is everybody missing me terribly?' I ask.

'I think people are afraid of me,' she says.

'They always were a bit, though, weren't they?'

'Yesterday, we all had to partner up for biology, and this one kid realised that she was going to be stuck with me and she went white. I said, "It's OK, I don't bite," but she went to the bathroom and didn't come back.'

'Were there Bunsen burners involved?'

'Yeah.'

'There you go. She probably thought you were going to blow her up.'

'Afterwards, I was standing on the landing in the science block. It was just after the bell went, and I'm looking down at the corridor and everyone's rushing around, going to their lockers and laughing and talking and being bored and all that, and none of them have a clue!'

'No-one knows. I can't believe that no-one knows.'

It's true. Seven and a half billion people nearly got chewed up by mutant alien insects and they have no idea. Why? Because Benny Doyle, that's why.

After we were arrested and charged and all that, we were allowed back home, and in the days after that, we waited impatiently for *them* to show up. The good guys. The people that sent Mam and Dad here in the first place.

The first thing Mam did after she reassured herself that myself and Dad were still alive was to send a message, to let *them* know what had happened, to let *them* know that the security ring had failed.

We figured that because so many people had seen the bugs in Oak Tree Heights, and because they'd caused so much damage, the cat was out of the bag. We expected what Dad called an 'engagement'. Like in films. A lot of spaceships appearing simultaneously in different parts of the world. The sudden revelation that we're not alone in the universe. We waited and waited but it didn't come.

Then, about a week after we were charged, Dad came into my bedroom looking all sheepish.

'What?' I said.

'There's a call for you.' And he produces a wristband just like Billy's.

I started at the sight of it. 'What's that? From who?'

He shrugged. 'My boss. She wants to talk to you. Alone.'

He showed me which button to press and left the room. Once he had closed the door, I picked the thing up. Just like Billy's. I pressed the button on the side and the hologram flared to life. A woman stood on the bedroom carpet, wearing some kind of grey military uniform. She was familiar looking.

'Hello, Martin. I am General Antel Io.'

It's funny. Before all this, I think I would have described her smile as 'kindly'. Now, though, I can only say that it *looked* kindly. It *seemed* kindly. She had been in the news hologram that we had seen in the mine, talking about how the eggs had been stolen.

'I am a member of the governing alliance here and I'm calling, in the first place, to apologise. We have let you all down very, very badly. You and your friends, and indeed your parents, should not have gone through what you went through. It was a failure on our part.' Her accent was just like Holly's.

'We're in a lot of trouble here, me and Tina,' I said.

'Yes, I understand that.'

'Are you going to come and explain what happened?'

She went silent for a moment. 'We have been monitoring the situation in Glencooper very closely over the last week, and we have reached a decision that we are not going to make our presence known at this time.'

'Oh, come on.'

'There are a number of reasons for this, Martin. The main reason is that we have found that early engagement with civilisations at Earth's stage of development have rarely ended well. I should say too that –'

'This is because of Benny Doyle, right?'

'I don't follow you.'

Benny Doyle. Glencooper's only native spacer. He was one of the people from Oak Tree Heights who saw the bugs. He was on his couch, binge watching *Firefly*, when the ground started shaking and car alarms started screaming. He grabbed his phone and dashed out the front door.

It also turns out that the bugs took out the power lines. I don't remember this happening, though I do remember the lights being out in the village. The moon was up at this stage, yes, but there wasn't really enough light to see anything by, so Benny's footage is just shadows and blurs and a lot of banging and shouting, along with Benny going 'Omigod, omigod, omigod,' and 'They're here, they're here, they're here,' about a million times.

So Benny, because he totally believes in UFOs and life on other planets and all that, realised what was going on instantly. This was an attack by mutant alien insects from outer space. But the other witnesses couldn't really believe what they were seeing. They'd just woken up and it was dark. They must have wondered if they were still dreaming. There was noise and confusion, but were there really giant killer insects flitting about the estate?

The following day, when Benny told everyone what had happened, they laughed at him. They told him that Spacer Sunday was over, that he needed to cop himself on and go back to work. He rang radio stations and newspapers and posted it all over the Internet, but no other witnesses came forward, and it's not hard to see why. When they saw everyone laughing at Benny and rolling their eyes and all that, they decided they didn't really want to be in the Benny camp. They began to doubt themselves. Giant insects? Hardly.

And all the damage in the estate? The tunnels that the bugs had burrowed up through? Someone suggested that the explosion at Kerrigan's quarry had somehow 'destabilised the mining network' and 'caused sinkholes'. Everyone swallowed this.

The thing is, there was no sign of the bugs anywhere, not so much as a bit of wing or the end of a leg. When they disappeared, they disappeared completely.

I explain all this to the hologram, who listens with no expression on her face at all.

'It's true, though, right? If everyone had seen those bugs and us shooting them down and all that, there'd be panic and you'd have to show up, right?'

'Martin, even if we did arrive, even if we did explain exactly what happened, there is no guarantee that you would avoid prosecution. It is not like getting a note from your parents to get out of gym class. And if we did intervene, it would be more or less impossible for you to remain anonymous. Believe it or not, this weighed heavily in our decision not to engage. Again, experience has taught us that the outcome for you would not be optimal.'

'So Tina and I have to go to jail.'

Again she paused. 'You don't know me, Martin, but I'm well-known here for being honest about how bad things may get. You may have to go to a detention home for a period of time. That is a possibility.'

'Well, you can tell Tina. I'm not going to.'

'But we know that we are to blame for what happened, and we plan to do everything in our power – short of intervening – to prevent that from happening. So there will be no shortage of legal and other resources made available to you and your parents to help ensure the best possible outcome. I have been briefed by our experts here and it is their view that you will avoid incarceration, though there are likely to be some punitive restrictions. You and Tina will bear the brunt of this. I'm not going to pretend you won't.'

In the end, between intergalactic legal advice and plenty of money for barristers, we stayed out of jail. They charged us with blowing up the quarry, but our legal team argued successfully that they couldn't prove it. In the end, we were convicted of dangerous driving, as well as the theft of the ambulance and the cop car. The judge gave us suspended sentences. We had to pretend we had driven the car – the one that Enda dematerialised – into the water and that we escaped in the turtle and were blown out to sea. Escaped in the turtle. Seriously.

Our legal people said that if we stayed apart – me and Tina – it would help convince the judge that we were serious about turning over new leaves and all that. So I volunteered to move school. Everything was harder for Tina. My parents at least understood why we did what we did. Obviously. But Tina's mother thinks that I led Tina astray. Me! I thought Mrs O'Reilly was laid-back. Turns out she's only laid-back until her daughter steals an ambulance and blows up a quarry. She's banned Tina from ever coming near me, which is why we meet up like this every Tuesday night.

'You sleeping much?' she says.

'Nah. You?'

'A bit.'

'Nightmares?'

'Oh yeah … but not about Enda's fall any more.'

'*You're* falling, I bet.'

'Sometimes. Or else I'm pottering around the house doing something ordinary; then I open a door and one of the bugs flies out at me.'

There's a noise behind us and we both jump.

'Enda!'

He drops the thing he's been dragging across the field and flops down on the blanket.

'You're late,' I say.

He leans back on his hands and stares out into the blackness, then says, 'Biscuit.'

I fish one out of the packet and hold it out to him. His arm rises unsteadily and he manages to grab it and direct it towards his mouth. Something glints in the darkness.

'Are you wearing your glasses again?'

The brain injury saved Enda from prosecution, even though stealing and destroying the cop car was one hundred per cent his idea. He's not back to himself, but he's getting there. That's the best thing about all of this. By far.

Tina jumps up, dusting down her clothes. 'Ready?'

'Yeah, give us a hand with this.'

It's the stupidest looking thing you ever saw. One long plank about thirty centimetres thick with three car seats fixed to it, one behind the other. We made it from stuff Tina's been collecting from the scrapyard near her house and depositing up here during the week. I drag it out until it's a few feet from the edge, and as I do, the clouds clear the moon again and everything turns pale and ghostly.

'I'll go in front,' says Tina. Enda shuffles into the middle seat and I help him with his seat belt. Then I take the back seat and strap myself in.

'You had your bananas?'

'Yeah.'

'One, two …' But I don't bother with three. We shoot off the edge of the cliff like a bullet out of a gun. I can hear Enda laughing as we fly past the top of the stack and race out over the sea. Tina's hands are in the air and she's screaming like she's on a roller coaster. I bring us slowly lower and lower until we're only inches above the surface of the water, so that I can reach down and feel the spray sting my hand. And then I bank slowly round and tilt us up so that we're aiming right at the moon, then, *Faster, faster, faster* and we're gone.

ACKNOWLEDGEMENTS

For all the help and support you've given me over the years, I want to thank my amazing wife Marie, and my wonderful, wonderful parents, known throughout the galaxies as Mam and Dad.

Also thank you to my brilliant squad of homegrown beta readers: Lily, Tom, Jim and Joni. Big love too to my fabulous sisters and brother: Eileen, Bridget, Eddie and Miriam.

ABOUT JOHN HEARNE

John Hearne was born in Wexford, Ireland, in 1970. He worked as an economist in Dublin before changing direction and becoming a freelance writer. He has ghost-written and edited a range of best-selling books, while his journalism has appeared in numerous national and international newspapers and magazines. His first middle grade novel, *The Very Dangerous Sisters of Indigo McCloud* was published by Little Island in 2021.

We hope you enjoyed reading
Someone's Been Messing with Reality.
On the following pages you can learn
about some other Little Island books
you might like to read.

THE WORDSMITH

by Patricia Forde — Laureate na nÓg
(Ireland's Children's Literature Laureate) 2023–26

**How many words
do you need to
survive?**

"Love", "hope",
"freedom" – in the
dystopian future of
Ark, after climate
change disaster,
these words are
being banned. One
girl takes a stand
against this loss of
language – she is
the Wordsmith.

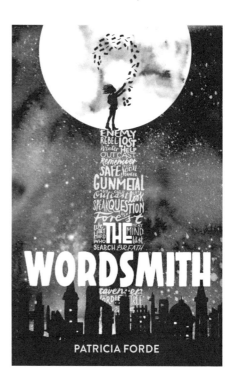

Winner of a White Raven Award from the
International Youth Library

A Library Association of America
Notable Book for Children

Over 60,000 copies sold worldwide

Published in the USA as *The List*

MOTHER TONGUE

by Patricia Forde — Laureate na nÓg
(Ireland's Children's Literature Laureate) 2023–26

After global warming came the Melting. Then came Ark.

The new dictator of Ark wants to silence speech for ever. But Letta is the Wordsmith, tasked with keeping words alive. Out in the woods, she and the rebels secretly teach children language, music and art.

Now there are rumours that babies are going missing. When Letta makes a horrifying discovery, she has to find a way to save the children of Ark – even if it is at the cost of her own life.

The sequel to the award-winning post-apocalypic novel *The Wordsmith*.

THE GIRL WHO FELL TO EARTH

*by Patricia Forde — Laureate na nÓg
(Ireland's Children's Literature Laureate) 2023–26*

Nobody can ever know Aria's secret: she has human DNA.

Raised on Planet Terros, Aria was taught to hate humans and their destructive ways. Now she and her father have been sent to Ireland to release a deadly virus and end the failed human experiment.

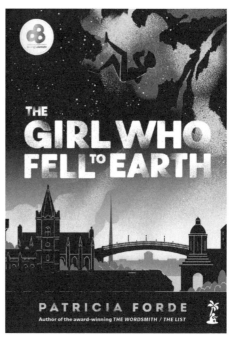

The mission goes wrong. Everything Aria thought she knew about Earth was a lie. And now forces from her past are out to destroy her.

Shortlisted for the Children's Books Ireland Awards 2024

"Suspenseful and thought-provoking." *Kirkus Reviews*

"An unmissable, thrilling sci-fi short read." *Irish Independent*

WILDLORD

by Philip Womack

'A writer of huge talent'
The Daily Telegraph

PHILIP
WOMACK

Something is menacing Mundham Farm. Does it come from outside – or within?

Who or what are the Samdhya, the supernatural people described in the old handwritten diaries Tom finds in his uncle's house?

As Tom starts to uncover the truth and learn new details about his parents' death, he is confronted with a stark choice: on the one hand, infinite power; on the other, freedom. Which will he choose?

"Womack is skilful at creating suspense." *Armadillo Magazine*

"If you're looking for a gripping adventure with a supernatural edge, this is just the ticket." *City Kids*

"Made me feel I was reading a classic from the shelves of my childhood." Jonathan Stroud

ABOUT LITTLE ISLAND

Little Island is an award-winning independent Irish publisher of books for young readers, founded in 2010 by Ireland's first Laureate na nÓg (children's laureate), Siobhán Parkinson. Little Island books are found throughout Ireland, the UK, North America, and in translation around the world. You can find out more at littleisland.ie

RECENT AWARDS FOR LITTLE ISLAND BOOKS

Youth Libraries Group Publisher of the Year 2023

British Book Awards 2024: Highly Commended

IBBY Honour List 2024
The Táin by Alan Titley, illus. by Eoin Coveney
Things I Know by Helena Close

An Post Irish Book Awards:
Teen and YA Book of the Year 2023
British Book Awards shortlist 2024
Black and Irish: Legends, Trailblazers & Everyday Heroes by Leon Diop and Briana Fitzsimons, illus. by Jessica Louis

An Post Irish Book Awards:
Children's Book of the Year (Senior) 2023
I Am the Wind: Irish Poems for Children Everywhere ed. by Sarah Webb and Lucinda Jacob, illus. by Ashwin Chacko

White Raven Award 2023
Carnegie Medal for Writing shortlist 2023
YA Book Prize shortlist 2023
Kirkus Prize finalist 2023
The Eternal Return of Clara Hart by Louise Finch